Hi ...

I'm Daizy Star, and I have a bit of a
problem. OK, make that a BIG problem.

It's my dad ... he's having a mid-life crisis
and it's seriously, seriously annoying. He
keeps getting these crazy ideas about
saving the world and, trust me, they are
the worst ideas in the history of the
universe. Bad times, huh?

At least I have my cool new pink guitar and
my dreams of rock superstardom to cling
to in the middle of this nightmare.

Who knows, music, friends and hot
chocolate with melted marshmallows might
just get me through ...

Love, hugs and custard doughnuts,

Daizy Star
(aged 11)

cathy cassidy

Daizy Star and the Pink Guitar

PUFFIN

PUFFIN BOOKS

Published by the Penguin Group
Penguin Books Ltd, 80 Strand, London WC2R 0RL, England
Penguin Group (USA) Inc., 375 Hudson Street, New York, New York 10014, USA
Penguin Group (Canada), 90 Eglinton Avenue East, Suite 700, Toronto, Ontario, Canada M4P 2Y3
(a division of Pearson Penguin Canada Inc.)
Penguin Ireland, 25 St Stephen's Green, Dublin 2, Ireland (a division of Penguin Books Ltd)
Penguin Group (Australia), 250 Camberwell Road, Camberwell, Victoria 3124, Australia
(a division of Pearson Australia Group Pty Ltd)
Penguin Books India Pvt Ltd, 11 Community Centre, Panchsheel Park, New Delhi – 110 017, India
Penguin Group (NZ), 67 Apollo Drive, Rosedale, North Shore 0632, New Zealand
(a division of Pearson New Zealand Ltd)
Penguin Books (South Africa) (Pty) Ltd, 24 Sturdee Avenue, Rosebank, Johannesburg 2196, South Africa

Penguin Books Ltd, Registered Offices: 80 Strand, London WC2R 0RL, England

puffinbooks.com

First published 2010
1

Text and illustrations copyright © Cathy Cassidy, 2010
All rights reserved

The moral right of the author/illustrator has been asserted

Set in Baskerville MT Standard 13/20pt
Made and printed in England by Clays Ltd, St Ives plc

British Library Cataloguing in Publication Data
A CIP catalogue record for this book is available from the British Library

ISBN: 978-0-141-32520-0

www.greenpenguin.co.uk

Mixed Sources
Product group from well-managed
forests and other controlled sources
www.fsc.org Cert no. SA-COC-1592
© 1996 Forest Stewardship Council.

Penguin Books is committed to a sustainable future
for our business, our readers and our planet.
The book in your hands is made from paper
certified by the Forest Stewardship Council.

1

My alarm clock goes off at 6.25 a.m. It sounds like a demented fire engine, only louder. I swat at it sleepily and it slides off the bedside table and lands on the floor with a *thud*.

'Ouch,' says a sleepy voice. 'Who threw that?'

I open one eye and come face to face with two feet, clad in pink fluffy socks. This is a little bit scary, until I remember I am sharing a bed with my best friend Beth. I wrestle her fluffy feet out of the way and peer down at my other best friend Willow, who is lying on the floor in a sleeping bag. She is still wearing the sparkly tiara and fairy wings she had on last night, and she is rubbing her head and trying to muffle the screeching alarm clock with a pillow at the same time.

1

'Sorry,' I tell her. 'I forgot you were there.'

I wriggle into a sitting position. My room, even in the half-light, looks like a bomb has hit it. The fairy lights that were draped around the curtain rail are hanging down to one side, still twinkling. The floor is littered with empty pizza boxes, crisp packets and Coke cans, and there's nothing left of the double choc chip muffins except a few crumbs and wrappers.

Last night was the best sleepover in the history of the universe, but this morning I'm feeling shell-shocked and sleepy, and Willow still hasn't managed to silence the alarm clock siren.

'What is that racket?' Beth wails, burrowing out from under the duvet with her blonde hair sticking up in clumps. 'It's making my ears hurt!'

'It's the alarm clock!' I say.

'I can't get it to stop,' Willow mutters, twiddling things and pressing buttons

and finally shaking it very, very hard. Still it shrieks on.

'Do something!' Beth howls. 'Pleeeease!'

So Willow does. She runs to the window, yanks it open and chucks the alarm clock out into the grey dawn sky. There is a satisfying *splash*, and then silence.

'I forgot next door had a pond,' she says in a small voice. 'Sorry, Daizy!'

Willow jumps under the covers with Beth and me, the sparkly tiara slightly askew over her dark braided hair. 'Why did it go off, anyway?' she grumbles. 'It's practically the middle of the night!'

'No, no, it's almost six thirty!' I say brightly. 'And that means –'

The bedroom door bursts open, and my family barge into the room in PJs and dressing gowns, whooping and cheering and firing party poppers at the ceiling.

'HAPPY BIRTHDAY, DAIZY STAR!' they

chorus, and then everyone starts singing, even
Willow and Beth.

It's sort of a tradition, you see – every year, on
3 November, my family get up and celebrate my
birthday at 6.30 because that is the exact time I
was born.

Eleven years ago exactly.

My little sister Pixie jumps on to the bed,
making Willow and Beth scream. She jumps up
and down, laughing, which really is not natural
for so early in the morning, and hands me a
still-soggy painting of
a glittery mermaid, a
wilted daisy chain and a
dark, solid, sunken
cake with watery white
icing and eleven
candles on top.

'Aw, thanks, Pixie!' I grin. 'Did you make the cake yourself?'

'Me and Dad did,' Pixie beams.

'Ah.'

If Dad was involved it means the cake is probably made of wholemeal, Fairtrade flour, with grated organic carrots and sprouted seeds and no sugar whatsoever. Yippee.

My dad is very keen on healthy eating, which is not always a good thing. It's a good job Mum was in charge of the food for the sleepover last night. She understands that birthday sleepovers need to involve pizza and crisps and Coke and muffins. I guess I can put up with a wholemeal birthday cake after all that lot.

I give Pixie a hug.

'My turn next,' my big sister Becca grins. She is already wearing pink eyeshadow, smudgy eyeliner and black lipstick, even though it is barely daybreak. It is hard work being a Goth. She hands me a parcel wrapped in black tissue paper, and I open it to reveal pink and black

fingerless gloves and a necklace made from black velvet ribbon with a silver skull and crossbones on it.

'Thank you, Becca,' I say. 'They're . . . um . . . lovely!'

And then I see that Mum and Dad are carrying presents too. Mum cradles a squarish parcel, while Dad hands me something long and heavy and wider at the bottom, wrapped in silver sparkly paper with a big red bow.

No matter how well it is wrapped, there is only one thing this present could possibly be. And it is something I have always dreamt of.

Well, for the last ten days, anyhow, ever since I spotted the bright pink electric guitar in the window of the music shop in town.

The minute I saw it, I knew that my star quality was destined to be music. At last, I would have a skill, a talent, a purpose in life! I could see myself strumming the pink guitar, writing cool songs and singing them, possibly on MTV. Or maybe just in the privacy of my bedroom –

hey, everyone has to start somewhere.

I dropped a lot of hints about the pink guitar, but I didn't dare hope I would really get it, not now Dad has given up his job and money is tight.

I fall on the silver sparkly paper and tear it off with shaking fingers, and there it is, just as I imagined, only better. The pink guitar!

'Cool!' says Beth.

'Awesome!' says Willow.

I launch myself off the bed and throw my arms round Mum and Dad. 'Wow!' I say. 'This is the best present I have ever had in my whole, entire life! Thank you!'

'We thought you should have what you wanted,' Mum says. 'Even though your dad is . . . um . . . between jobs. Becca had a nice birthday

present, and Pixie had her swimming party . . .
We wanted to be fair.'

'And there's a teeny-tiny scratch on the back,
so we got twenty-five pounds off,' Pixie adds
helpfully.

I don't care about the teeny-tiny scratch,
or the discount. I run my fingertips over the
shiny paintwork, *twang* one of the strings. It
feels good.

'You can be a rock star now,' Pixie tells me.

'Yeah, right!' I laugh.

'I could show you a few chords,' Dad suggests.
'I was quite good on the guitar, back in my
student days.'

'Hmmm, I remember,' Mum says tactfully.
'I expect we could get you some lessons, Daizy.'

The squarish parcel turns out to be a little
amp, and Dad shows me how to plug the guitar
in and strum. A loud, crackly, jangling noise
floods the bedroom and everyone except Becca
clamps their hands over their ears.

'Lessons would be a good idea,' Beth frowns.

'Oh, I don't know . . . that sounded great!'
Becca says.

If Becca likes it, I definitely need lessons. And
if playing guitar is going to be my star quality, I
had better get started right away.

'Anyway,' Dad says, 'happy birthday, Daizy.
Eleven years old!'

Mum leans down and lights the birthday
candles, and another chorus of 'Happy Birthday'
erupts as I blow out the candles, laughing.

'Make a wish!' Pixie squeals.

I close my eyes and wish hard. I'm wishing
that this year will be the year I finally find my
talent, the one thing I'm really good at, the thing
that makes me shine. Eleven would be a good age
to discover that.

All the time I'm wishing, I hug the pink guitar
close. Please, please let this be it . . .

2

Birthday cake for breakfast is almost always a good thing . . . unless the cake is sunken and solid, with all the flavour of a wholemeal house brick. I gnaw on my slice politely, curled up on the sofa playing Pictionary with Beth and Pixie while Willow stretches out on the carpet, playing a computer game on Dad's laptop.

If Mum was here, she'd dispose of the cake quickly and quietly and whip up something yummy, but sadly, she's on early shift at the hospital today.

'This looks delicious . . .' Beth tells Pixie

kindly, selecting the smallest possible piece. 'You
are clever!'

'It's easy,' Pixie shrugs. 'Just like making mud
pies, really!'

'Mud pies?' Beth blinks, then slides her plate
out of sight behind the sofa when she thinks
nobody is looking.

'But with stewed dates and roasted linseeds
instead of mud, of course,' Pixie reassures her.
'Dad says they are superfoods, designed to make
you glow with health. I'm glad you like it.'

'It's very . . . um . . . unusual,' Beth says
weakly.

My little sister takes a piece of cake and bites
into it, grinning. Then her face crumples. 'It's all
gritty!' she howls, throwing down the cake in
disgust. 'Ugh!'

'That'll be the roasted linseeds,' I sigh. 'Never
mind, Pixie. This healthy-eating kick of Dad's is
a nightmare. I wish he'd just get back to normal.'

'Normal' is not a word you could use about
my dad, though. Not lately, anyhow. Ever since

his job as a geography teacher at a
ry school a while back, he has been
rangely indeed.

My big sister Becca says it is a mid-life crisis.

If you don't know what a mid-life crisis is, then
trust me, you are very, very lucky, because it is
NOT a good thing. It's actually quite sad and
tragic, and deeply annoying at the same time.

Becca says that some men have a mid-life crisis
when they get to about forty and realize they are
getting old and grey and wrinkly, so I expect
that's what has happened to Dad. He keeps
having these deeply scary ideas for making his
dreams come true, which is bad news because
Dad's dreams are a bit like everyone else's
nightmares.

'Let's bin it,' Pixie decides. 'Dad will never
know!'

Dad is out on his morning run, which means
we are safe for a while, so I tip the remains of the
yucky cake into the outside bin. I hope that this
won't affect my birthday wish coming true.

I run upstairs and knock on Becca's bedroom door.

'Yeah?' she yells over the racket of clashy, trashy punk music. I step inside. Becca's room is a twilight zone of black and red net and wall-to-wall posters of scary-looking bands. Becca is sitting on the bed, painting her fingernails black.

'Becca . . .' I say. 'Bit of a problem. We tried to eat the cake Dad and Pixie made . . .'

'Ouch,' Becca says, rolling her eyes. She reaches under the bed and pulls out her emergency jar of instant hot chocolate, along with a bag of marshmallows. My big sister is a great believer in the healing powers of hot chocolate, and luckily she is also very good at sharing.

The two of us are in the kitchen, dropping marshmallows on to steaming mugs of hot chocolate, when the doorbell rings.

'Surprise!' says Murphy Malone, my best boy mate. He is standing on the doorstep carrying a plate piled high with custard doughnuts, with random birthday candles flickering in the November breeze. 'I wasn't sure what to get you, so I just took the easy option . . .'

'It's perfect!' I tell him. I blow the candles out because I am not about to miss a second chance to make my wish come true and discover my star quality. Then I drag Murphy into the living room where Beth, Willow and Pixie fall on the doughnut mountain like a pack of starving wolves, with Becca and me close behind.

Custard doughnuts and hot chocolate . . . now *that's* a birthday breakfast.

Murphy lives just over the street from me – we've been friends for ages. He is not all annoying like some boys I could mention. He is into cool clothes and funny haircuts and bands that nobody else has heard of, and he's kind and funny and has never, ever put a worm down the back of my sweatshirt, the way Ethan Miller did back in Year Three. He also has a serious addiction to custard doughnuts, which is obviously very useful at moments like these.

'So . . .' Murphy asks, licking the sugar off his lips. 'How was the girly sleepover?'

'Great,' I say. 'We stayed up till midnight watching Disney DVDs. We painted our toenails every colour of the rainbow and dressed up in tiaras and fairy wings, eating pizza and choc chip muffins. And this morning, Willow chucked my alarm clock in the pond. The usual, really.'

'Er . . . cool,' Murphy says. 'I think.'

'It was. Have you seen what Mum and Dad got me?' I pick up the pink guitar and strum a long rock solo, shaking my head about so that my hair whirls around like a whole bunch of snakes doing the hula. Luckily, the amp is not plugged in this time, so Murphy doesn't have to cover his ears.

'Looks amazing,' Murphy says, biting into his fourth custard doughnut. 'You should start a band!'

'Oh, I will!' I tell him, grinning. 'As soon as I've learnt to play!'

Willow looks at her watch. 'Mum will be here to pick me up soon,' she says. 'Shall I shut this laptop down?'

I flop down on to the floor beside her.

'I'll do it.' I click a couple of times, then frown as I spot a file I've never seen before on Dad's laptop. It says *Africa Project*. A little niggle of worry unravels inside me.

Of course, an ex-geography teacher has every right to have a file on his laptop called *Africa Project*. It is probably crammed with dusty old graphs on the rainfall of the Kalahari Desert and essays on farming in the Congo – nothing but yawn-making facts. Probably.

But then again, nothing Dad does is normal any more. I can't help remembering his last crazy plan.

Before I can help myself, I click the file open. Inside are lots of documents about a place called Malawi. It looks a lot like a geography teacher's research project. When I open one of the documents, the screen fills with photos. A vast blue lake, a scorching savannah, smiling villagers in bright print wraps, and image after image of lions, elephants, leopards, rhinos . . .

Beth, Willow, Murphy, Pixie and Becca crowd round the screen.

'Wow,' Beth says. 'Is your dad planning a holiday? A safari?'

'Doubt it,' Becca huffs. 'We just don't *do* holidays like that. We had a day trip to Eastbourne this summer, remember?'

'But he's changed lately,' Willow reminds us. 'He's got all adventurous, hasn't he?'

'Kind of,' I admit uneasily.

'He wants to travel and see the world,' Pixie chips in.

That's definitely true. Dad talks a lot about getting out of the rat race and following his dreams. A long-haul holiday to Africa might be exactly the kind of thing he would plan, now he is in the grip of the mid-life crisis. Mightn't it?

Before we have time to discuss any more, Dad comes in from his run, wobbly and purple-faced. 'Hello, kids!' he gasps. 'Anyone for a nice wheatgrass and celery smoothie?'

'No thanks,' I say quickly. I've tried Dad's wheatgrass and celery smoothies before. They taste like something you might use to clean the sink.

'Dad . . .' Pixie says. My little sister is bursting with excitement. In her shining eyes I can see visions of giraffes and wildebeest, lions and leopards. 'Dad . . . are we *really* going on a safari holiday to Africa?'

The smile freezes on Dad's face as he sees the

open laptop, the photos and files. He is looking shifty now, as well as purple-faced.

'Um . . . not exactly a safari holiday . . .' he admits.

Pixie's shoulders slump, and Becca folds her arms, her face stern.

'I can explain,' Dad says. 'I wasn't going to mention it yet, not until things were definite, but . . .'

Beth, Willow and Murphy look at Dad brightly, waiting for the explanation. But me? Seriously, I do not want to know. There's a cold, sour swirl of fear in my tummy that tells me I'm not going to like this.

I'm not going to like it at all.

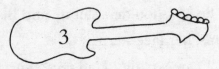

3

I think I might just hang upside down on the old tyre-swing in the park, possibly for the rest of my life. Trust me, the world looks better that way.

My long hair trails along the grass, and the blue sky swings violently above me. Every now and again, a crispy, red-gold leaf drifts down from the top of the big tree the tyre-swing is dangling from, and I reach out a hand to catch one because it's lucky to catch a falling leaf.

Needless to say, I don't catch any.

Dad has had another Crazy Idea, and this one is so crazy I don't even want to think about it. I just want to hang upside down on the tyre-swing

until it all goes away, but
that's not a good idea, I
know. Pretty soon, my legs
will start to ache and I will
land in a heap on the grass, with
a sore head and bruises to add to
my troubles.

'Are you coming down?'
Murphy asks, leaning against the
tree.

'No,' I tell him. 'My life is
over.'

'Nah,' he tells me. 'Your
dad's just dreaming again.
This whole Africa thing will
never happen. It'll fizzle out, just
like his last big idea. Come down, Daizy,
and we can talk about it. Don't bury your head
in the sand.'

'What sand?' I ask.

'You know what I mean,' Murphy says. 'You have to face facts. No running away from the truth, OK?'

'I am not running away,' I say reasonably. 'I'm just trying to see things from a different perspective.'

This sounds pretty good, I think, even though I'm not too sure what it means.

I swing a while longer, looking at Murphy. He looks especially wise and kind and cool upside down, with his red skinny jeans and toilet-brush hair.

I will miss Murphy Malone.

My eyes brim with tears. They roll down over my forehead and into my hair, which feels a little strange.

Suddenly, I tip backwards on to the grass, landing with a bump. 'Ouch!' I say.

Murphy sits down beside me. 'Usually,' he says, 'I'd suggest custard doughnuts at a time like this. They never fail to make me feel better, no matter what. But today . . . well, I guess we've

overdosed on the doughnuts already.'

'We have a bit,' I admit. 'More would be a bad idea.'

'Very bad,' Murphy agrees. 'Imagine if your teeth went black and fell out, Daizy, on top of the whole Africa thing!'

I glare at him. 'Yes, imagine. I thought you were meant to be making me feel better, not worse.'

'Sorry,' Murphy says.

I am not sure if anything can make me feel

better, but maybe Murphy is right – I have to face facts.

My dad is not planning a safari holiday to Africa at all. That would be too simple, too much like fun. No, he is planning to take the whole family to live in this place called Malawi, to build a school and dig a well and grow mangoes, or whatever people grow out there.

You heard me right . . . to LIVE.

I mean, Malawi is probably a very beautiful place and everything, but I don't want to LIVE there! I want to live here, in Brightford, where I have good friends and the best schoolteacher in the universe, where there are tyre-swings and custard doughnuts and bright pink electric guitars.

When Dad unveiled his terrible plan, I pretty much froze with horror. Even Beth and Willow were speechless, and trust me, that doesn't happen very often. They know how upset I was last time Dad cooked up something like this, after all, and they tried to get Dad to see sense. It was a waste of breath, of course. My dad wouldn't see sense if it was jumping up and down in front of him, wearing neon-pink pyjamas.

'You're going to live in Malawi?' Willow said bravely. 'Isn't that a bit drastic? I think a safari holiday would be much more fun.'

'I don't think you quite understand,' Dad had said.

'I don't think I do, either,' I argued. 'I mean, it's probably very nice out there, but don't they have snakes and lions and leopards and poisonous spiders? It could be dangerous!'

But Dad wasn't listening. He launched into a speech about helping others and sharing skills and making a difference. When Willow's mum turned up to take Willow home and drop Beth off on the way, my two best friends hugged me tightly and told me not to worry, they'd think of something.

And then it was just Becca, Pixie, Murphy, Dad and me.

'I've got it all planned out,' Dad told us. 'I've

already contacted some of the charities who send volunteers to Malawi, and they are crying out for teachers and nurses. There's an amazing project about to start in a village called Tatu Mtengo. It would be perfect for us! I could teach, and your mum could be the village nurse. And you three kids could go to school as normal, but in a whole new culture. Think of it! You'll soon pick up the language . . . Chichewa, most of the locals speak, but English is widely spoken too. You'll be living close to nature, experiencing life in the African bush at first hand. Fetching the water, picking the maize, grinding the millet, milking the goats –'

'Goats?' I echoed weakly. 'Does Mum know about this?'

'Um . . . not exactly,' Dad bluffed. 'Not yet. But once I explain it, she's going to just love the idea!'

'Don't count on it!' Becca had growled. She gave Dad a look that could wither an oak tree, then stomped up the stairs to her room and turned her music up so high it made the ceiling shake. I felt a bit bad about using up her emergency hot chocolate supplies this morning because she was probably needing them now.

Still, she had the right idea, my big sister. She was making it clear, right from the start, that she was not impressed. I knew how she felt. I did not want to stand around listening to Dad drone on about goat-keeping in Africa.

I'd had more than enough of my dad's mad ideas just lately. I shot Murphy a worried look and turned towards the front door.

'Can I have my own lion cub?' Pixie was asking chirpily, as I strode along the garden path with Murphy at my heels. 'Or a meerkat and a warthog, like Timon and Pumbaa in *The Lion King*?'

'Um, not sure you can keep lion cubs as pets, Pixie, love,' Dad muttered. 'Daizy! Daizy, come back! Where are you going?'

'Malawi,' I said under my breath, and slammed the gate behind me.

Now, I am sitting on the grass in the park with Murphy at my side, trying to make sense of it all.

'I love my dad,' I tell Murphy glumly.

'I know,' he says.

'But I do not want to go to Malawi and fetch water from the well and pick maize and milk goats in the African sun. It is not the kind of birthday surprise I had in mind.'

'I know,' he says again.

'It's just a really, really, REALLY bad idea!'

'I know,' Murphy sighs.

I jump to my feet, hands on hips. You cannot run away from a thing like this. Like Murphy said, you cannot bury your head in the sand, or hang upside down on a tyre-swing for the rest of your life. Some disasters have to be faced head-on.

'Murphy?' I say.

'Mmmm?'

'This is not happening. I am going to stop it.'

I am going to stop Dad from dragging us over to the other side of the world and ruining our lives. I will find a way, even if it kills me. I just have to work out how.

4

Luckily, I am eleven years old now. I am very nearly grown-up, and quite wise and mature compared to when I was ten and three-quarters.

When a disaster unfolds right in the middle of my living room, which seems to happen quite a lot these days, I am not about to run for cover, screaming. I am not about to pretend it isn't happening or try to keep it secret or lie awake for long hours all through the night, tossing and turning and having stomach-churning nightmares, like I did with Dad's last big plan.

No, those days are gone.

Slamming gates and hanging upside down on tyre-swings will not cut it, either.

I am eleven now, and I am going to deal with this problem in a mature and sensible way. I will stay calm at all times, and listen, and gather information. The more I know, the more I can do to stop this whole thing from happening.

I even have a notebook, so I can jot down important points and then use them to come up with a plan later.

While I was out at the park, Dad made some cabbage and kidney-bean soup for tea, with the misguided idea that this will cheer us up and win us over to his cause. Yeah, right. Anyway, now he is happily stirring it, filling us in on the little details of his big African dream.

Becca is yelling that Dad is a deranged lunatic whose only dream is to rip our lives into tiny shreds and scatter them to the four winds, and Pixie is still trying to decide whether she would rather have a zebra or an anteater as a pet.

Mum is sitting at the kitchen table, head in hands, shoulders shaking. I worried at first that she was crying, but no, she is laughing. In a slightly alarming kind of way. I am starting to think that I am the only sane one in my whole family, when thankfully Mum says something distinctly un-crazy.

'Africa?' Mum says, shaking her head in disbelief. 'You want us to abandon everything and go to live in Africa so you can build a school and dig a well and keep a herd of goats?'

School, I write. *Well. Herd of goats.*

'Mike,' Mum smirks. 'Have you gone mad?'

'What's mad about it?' Dad asks, puzzled, and Mum just rolls her eyes.

'We have a nice home here. I have a job – a job that is keeping us afloat, by the way, now that you have decided you don't want to be a teacher any more,' Mum says patiently. 'The girls have school, and good friends. And none of us – NONE of us, Mike – except you . . . want to go and live in Africa. Not right now. OK?'

'We cannot put our lives on hold, waiting for the right time!' Dad says. 'We have to do this NOW. Malawi needs us. Think of what we could do! We have skills, Livvi, skills that could really help an African village. I can teach . . . teach kids who truly want to learn. You can nurse and save lives, help children to grow up strong and healthy. Can't you see what a difference you could make?'

Mum frowns. 'I know, but that's not the point . . .'

'What is the point, Livvi?' Dad demands. 'What do you really want from life? Money? Status? A flat-screen TV? Or would you like to know that you had saved lives, made a difference to the world?'

'A new TV would be quite nice,' Pixie muses. 'We could watch my *Little Mermaid* DVD on it.'

'There won't be any TV in rural Malawi,' Becca snaps, and Pixie's lower lip quivers a little.

'Livvi?' Dad repeats. 'Voluntary work was always a dream of yours, before the kids came along. You cared. You wanted to make a difference.'

'I know,' Mum says. 'I still do. I mean, I'd like to, of course, but –'

'No buts, Livvi,' Dad says. 'Just consider it, that's all I'm asking. All of you. I am asking you a difficult thing, I know. I am asking you to think about others, not yourselves. Is that too much to ask?'

'Think about others?' Becca squeaks, outraged. 'Think about OTHERS? When do YOU ever think about others, Dad? You cook up these crazy ideas and expect us to go along with them, but you never, ever think about how we might feel!'

There are tears streaming down Becca's face, making her eyeliner run into rivulets of black.

'I want what's best for you!' Dad argues. 'This would be the experience of a lifetime! Yes, there would be challenges, but you'll thank me one day, I promise you!'

'Wanna bet?' Becca growls.

'There are health risks to consider,' Mum points out. 'We'd have to have lots of jabs, and take malaria tablets every day. Is that fair on the kids?'

Malaria, I write in my notebook, feeling slightly alarmed.

'Life isn't fair!' Dad says with passion, setting the table with soup bowls and spoons. 'Do you think it is fair for the children of Malawi? Do you know what those children would DO for a bowlful of this lovely cabbage and kidney-bean soup?'

Becca whirls round, lifts the steaming soup pan from the cooker and chucks the whole lot down the sink.

'Stuff your disgusting cabbage soup!' she yells, in between sobs. 'Stuff your kidney beans! I hate you! I am not going to live in Malawi and milk goats every morning, and that is final!'

Stuffed kidney beans, I write.

Things are starting to look kind of bleak. Becca has stormed off to her room, and Mum has marched upstairs to change and run a relaxing bubble bath to calm her nerves. Pixie is in the living room, watching a DVD of *The Lion King* to prepare herself for life in Africa.

Dad looks at me across the table, sad-eyed and glum.

'What about you, Daizy?' he asks. 'Do you think I'm crazy too?'

'Um . . . only a little bit,' I tell him. 'Don't worry about Becca. She is very dramatic these days. I think it's her hormones. Or maybe something to do with being a Goth?'

'Maybe,' Dad sighs. 'I'm just trying to follow my dreams. Is that so wrong?'

'Um . . .'

'Your mum and Becca are not convinced,' he says. 'I wish I could make them understand. At least you and Pixie are more open-minded, more adventurous, willing to give things a go.'

'Er . . . right,' I mutter. If Dad knew I was plotting to overthrow his plan, what would he think then? I smile guiltily and Dad ruffles my hair, the way he used to when I was Pixie's age.

I haven't the heart to tell Dad that this dream

has even less chance of happening than the last one. How can it? Mum is not crazy about the idea of living in Malawi and Becca is outraged at the very idea of it. I let out a little sigh of relief. It's not going to happen, surely . . . not when Mum is so firmly against it all.

'What have you been writing down?' Dad asks, spotting my notebook.

I close it quickly.

'Nothing,' I say. 'Just making a list of . . . um . . . useful things for Malawi.'

Dad's face lights up. 'That's my girl,' he grins. 'I knew you would understand. I just knew I could count on you, Daizy Star!'

Oops.

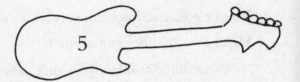

5

I am in love.

    I know it's love because my heart is racing and whole flocks of butterflies are doing triple somersaults in my tummy.

Beth and Willow said this would happen. They said it was inevitable, a part of growing up, and that I had better watch out now I was eleven because my hormones would be bubbling away like one of Dad's nettle and wheatgrass smoothies. I mean, ewwww! And then just when I least expect it, *BAM*! I'd be in love.

This happened to Beth and Willow earlier in the term, with Ethan Miller. He is without doubt the yuckiest boy I have ever met, the kind who spends hours in front of the mirror perfecting his hair-gelled spikes and playing with his mum's fake tan. Ugh. His only skills are football and winding people up.

Still, you cannot choose who you fall for, I suppose. And now I have fallen too, head over heels, just like Beth and Willow said I would. They assumed it would be with a boy, of course, but who says you can't fall in love with a pink guitar?

After all, a boy might let you down, but a guitar never would. It stays faithful and true to the end, and it's always there when you want to let off steam. And this weekend, obviously, there has been a lot of steam.

It is kind of tragic, really. I am discovering my star quality, I'm sure I am – and now perhaps it could be snatched away from me forever. Who knows, maybe I am swapping a future as the world's most talented rock princess for a life of milking goats under the blistering African sun.

In between writing tragic rock songs about living in a tin hut on the shores of Lake Malawi, I have spent hours and hours on the Internet, researching life in Africa.

It hasn't really helped me to come up with a plan to stop Dad's mad idea. It has just made me feel very, very gloomy.

'Did you know that Malawi is one of the poorest countries in the world?' I ask Beth and Willow, next day at school.

'You might have mentioned it,' Beth says patiently.

'Once or twice,' Willow sighs.

We are in the school lunch hall, eating sausage and mash with baked beans. I bet they don't have *that* in Malawi.

'I can understand why Dad wants to go over and help,' I tell my friends. 'I mean, some villages have no clean water at all. They have all these scary diseases and there aren't enough hospitals

40

or clinics or medical supplies to make people better, or even enough doctors and nurses. And there aren't enough schools or teachers for kids like us to have a proper education . . .'

'Lucky things,' says Ethan Miller, leaning over to spear a sausage from my plate. 'No school! Just imagine!'

I slap his hand, and the stolen sausage plummets down into the water jug, where it sinks without trace.

'Ouch,' he says.

'It's not funny, Ethan!' I growl. 'How would you like it if you had to work in the fields all day long in the scorching sun, just to help your family put food on the table? How would you like not being able to read or write?'

Ethan shrugs. I should have guessed. Reading and writing is no big deal to a boy like him.

'Do they have football over there?' he asks.

'No!' I snap, although I think they probably do. Football is the kind of stupid game that finds its way just about everywhere.

Ethan blinks. 'No football?' he gasps. 'That's terrible!'

Beth flutters her eyelashes at him sweetly. 'That's what Daizy is trying to tell you,' she explains. 'Malawi is a developing country, and Daizy's dad wants to go out there and help.'

'Help?' Ethan echoes.

'Yes, help,' Willow explains, a little breathlessly, squinting at Ethan. 'He wants to build a school, dig a well, teach the kids.'

Willow was reading my sister Becca's *TeenGal* magazine at the sleepover. There was a feature called 'Flirting For Beginners', with tips for speaking softly and sending lots of mushy glances towards the one you love. Willow needs a bit more practice with the glances. A lot more, actually.

'Er . . . cool,' Ethan says. 'He could teach them football, right?'

'Right,' Willow squints.

'Have you got something in your eye?' Ethan asks.

Willow stops squinting and rolls her eyes up to the ceiling in exasperation. 'No, I have not,' she sighs. 'Do you want my sausage?'

It didn't say anything in *TeenGal* about sausages as a flirting technique, but it seems to do the trick with Ethan Miller. He grabs the sausage and swallows it down in three bites, and Beth offers him hers too. It's kind of sad to see your two best friends fussing and flirting around a footy-mad bonehead like Ethan Miller, but they say love is blind.

'And Daizy's mum is a nurse,' Willow rushes on. 'So she could be really useful too. The whole family might have to go over.'

'To Malawi?' Ethan blinks.

'To Malawi,' Beth sighs. 'It sucks, right?'

Ethan frowns. He actually looks slightly upset, but that may just be because I made him drop the stolen sausage into the water jug, of course. Not because he would miss me, or anything. Ethan Miller is not that kind of boy. He is probably just wondering who else he could wind up and annoy, if I ended up living in Malawi.

'It's not definite,' I say. 'I don't suppose it will really happen. Mum doesn't seem too keen.'

I push my plate away and reach for the bowl of steaming sponge pudding and chocolate sauce. Mmmm . . . I take one bite, but the warm, sweet sponge seems to stick in my throat. A pudding like this could keep a whole family in Malawi going for a week, probably.

I put my spoon down again, tasting guilt instead of chocolate.

Ethan is digging me in the ribs. 'I could bring in a spare football from home, if that would help?' he suggests. 'For the kids over there.'

I glare at him. 'The kids in Malawi don't need footballs, they need schools and hospitals and wells and herds of goats!'

'Goats?' Ethan puzzles. 'What do goats have to do with it?'

'A herd of goats can keep a whole bunch of families in food and milk for years and years!' I say. 'Not to mention providing manure to help grow vegetables, and skins to make shoes and things.'

'My uncle keeps goats,' Ethan says. 'He makes this really disgusting cheese.'

Cheese? I worry about Ethan Miller, sometimes. He has a brain like a grasshopper.

'Maybe I could bring you in a goat?' Ethan muses.

'Don't be stupid,' I snap. Ethan just doesn't get it. He thinks he can fix everything with an old football and a goat. As if it could be that simple. 'What use is one measly little goat? You'd need a whole herd of them . . .'

I trail away into silence. I can feel little cogs and wheels creaking away inside my brain, slowly, painfully. It couldn't be that simple . . . could it?

'That's it!' I grin at Ethan. 'That's what I have to do! Raise the money to buy a herd of goats and dig a well and get medical supplies and school books and everything! And if I can do all of that, then maybe, just maybe, Dad will decide we don't have to go out there!'

Beth is frowning. 'Daizy,' she says patiently. 'You're talking about hundreds and hundreds of pounds! How are you going to get that kind of money?'

'I don't know,' I say. 'But I'll think of something!'

'I hope so,' Willow says. 'I don't want you to go and live in Malawi.'

'Me neither,' Beth agrees.

'Nor me,' Ethan Miller adds.

Beth, Willow and I turn together and give him a long, hard stare. Ethan winks at me, and just for a moment I wonder if it would actually be worth living in Malawi for a year, just to get away from the most annoying boy in the whole, entire world.

As for the winking, that will have to stop right now. I don't want Beth and Willow getting the wrong idea about me and Ethan Miller, like they did at the start of term when they thought I fancied him.

I mean . . . eeewwww!

This time, though, Beth and Willow just smile. Beth flutters her eyelashes, and Willow gives him that squinty look again and links an arm through his.

'Don't worry, Ethan,' she says in that breathless, whispery voice. 'We won't let anything happen to Daizy.'

'No way,' Beth adds. 'The three of us can work together to come up with a plan.'

Ethan looks slightly alarmed, but you do not argue with Beth and Willow. They tow him off towards the playground, plotting and whispering, and I am left alone in an empty lunch hall. I look down at my dish of sponge pudding and chocolate sauce.

It's cold and soggy and disappointing, just like my life.

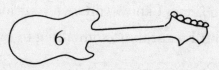

6

Dad does not seem to be giving up on his Malawi dreams. I think he is trying to wear Mum down, win her over to the idea, but so far it doesn't seem to be working.

'Isn't it what everybody wants in life?' he says. 'To say they have made a difference? Changed things for the better? Helped other people?'

'You don't have to go to Malawi to do that,' Mum huffs. 'I do those things every day, at work. It's what a nurse does.'

Well, I suppose so. I can see it is not quite what Dad has in mind, though. Mum has just been telling us about one of her patients, who managed to nick a wheelchair and make a break

for freedom, returning half an hour later with
fish, chips and chocolate bars for the whole ward.

'You can't blame him,' Mum had said.
'Hospital food is not the best.'

'Livvi, I know you love your job,' Dad says.
'But I want to do something to make a difference
too.'

'You did, when you were teaching,' Mum says.

'The children at Green Lane Community
School did not want to be changed,' Dad
grumbles. 'They just wanted to send text
messages under the desk and read copies of
Hello magazine whenever my back was turned.
They were beyond help.'

'Nobody is beyond help,' Mum tells him, but
I think she could be wrong. I think that Dad
might be.

'Malawi needs us,' he says with passion, and
Becca throws her maths homework in the bin
and says that if Dad doesn't give up on the whole
idea, she is going to run off with her boyfriend
Spike and join the circus.

'We've been planning it,' she says. 'We will be the first Goth trapeze artistes ever. Or maybe we will do a high-wire act, or ride unicycles. But we will definitely do it, Dad, unless you come to your senses.'

Dad fishes the maths book out of the bin, brushing off a couple of beansprouts, but Becca says she won't need to know about advanced geometry when she is in the circus.

Mum sighs. 'Don't worry, Becca. Nobody is going to Malawi.'

'Don't worry, Becca,' Dad echoes. 'You'll love Africa. We all will. Just give this idea a chance!'

The door slams so hard it makes the floor shake. I am used to seeing Becca flounce off to her room, but this time it isn't Becca.

It's Mum.

If there is one thing worse than living in a tin hut in Malawi with a herd of goats for company, it is watching my parents row. It is not nice. It makes my tummy churn with worry, and my mouth turn down at the sides.

I would rather pack my bag tomorrow and head for Africa than listen to any more slamming doors and huffy arguments.

Luckily, I have the pink guitar to focus on. I took it to school yesterday, to show Miss Moon. I had been hoping she might ask me to do a guitar solo in front of the whole class, and then give me her special Star of the Week award for being a musical genius, but sadly, no. Tom Taylor got the Star of the Week award, for building a model of the Eiffel Tower out of matchsticks. It was pretty amazing.

Miss Moon did say my guitar was lovely, and told me I was a very lucky girl. Then she suggested we put it in her stock cupboard for safekeeping. I guess my plans to wow the school with my rock princess performance will have to wait.

★

On Friday, Mum announces that she has signed me up for a course of guitar lessons with a famous guitar guru called Mr Tingley.

I practically jump up and down with excitement.

'Are you sure that's a good idea, Livvi?' Dad asks. 'There's not much point in Daizy starting guitar lessons now. We might not be here for much longer.'

My heart sinks. 'I'd really like lessons,' I say in a very small voice. 'Please?'

'You won't *need* an electric guitar in Malawi,' Dad says.

'I will!' I protest. 'I will need it wherever I go! What if I get inspired and need to write a song?'

'Of course she will need her guitar!' Becca defends me. 'Get real, Dad. Don't you even *care* that you are turning our lives upside down?'

'Try to see it as an adventure,' Dad grins. 'Most of the schemes I'm looking at are just for a year. We can all manage for a year without guitars and TV and hot and cold running water, right? One year, that's all I ask!'

'But a year is like forever!' Becca argues.

'Just give it a chance,' Dad insists. 'We would never regret it! The chance to give something back, to change things for the better, to leave the world a better place than we found it . . .'

'Leave the world?' I repeat, horrified. 'You mean we could DIE?'

'No, no, that's not what I mean at all!' Dad huffs. 'I just mean –'

'We'll talk about it later,' Mum says firmly. 'OK, Mike? About the health and safety aspects, and education, and the culture shock, and whether it would be the best thing for us all, as a family. Calm down, everybody. It is most unlikely we are going anywhere, OK?'

I stare at Mum, wide-eyed. She is not the kind of mum who yells and argues and gets stroppy. She is gentle and kind and easy-going. Last time Dad had a crazy idea, she complained a bit, but mostly she just went along with it until he realized it was a bad, bad plan.

This time around, though, she looks very grumpy and cross. She doesn't want to go to Malawi any more than we do – and she is making sure Dad knows it.

'As for Daizy, of course she should have guitar lessons,' she says. 'It's all arranged. OK?'

'OK,' I say in a small voice. 'Thanks.'

Later, much later, when I'm lying in bed with the stars shining in through the gap in my curtains, I hear Mum and Dad downstairs, arguing. Their raised voices drift up through the darkness, spiky, grating, awkward. I pull the duvet over my head, but still those voices worm their way in. They get inside my head. They make my eyes mist with tears and my tummy ache.

Mum and Dad never used to argue.

What if Mum decides she has had enough of Dad's crazy plans? What if my family falls to pieces?

I can't even bear to think about it. Anything would be better than that.

Even Malawi.

7

A week later I am sitting in the waiting room of Mr Tingley's Guitar Studio, cradling the pink guitar and waiting for my first lesson. I am nervous, but in a good way. It is like being at the start of a very exciting journey that could end with fame, fortune or, at the very least, a Star of the Week award.

Mr Tingley will spot my raw talent and train me to become a rock legend.

Well, maybe.

Spotting talent may not be his strong point.

Right now, the sound of screeching guitar strings booms through the studio door, making my ears hurt. The racket builds into a frenzy of strangled, mangled chords before ending with a series of slamming *thuds* that sounds like guitars and amps being smashed to bits. This is a bit worrying. Have I come to the right place?

The studio door opens and a tall, black-clad Goth boy slouches out, lugging a guitar. His lip-piercing glints in the light, and he peers menacingly from behind a dipping, green-dyed fringe as he looms over me.

I blink.

'Hello, Daizy,' he says.

'Hello, Spike! I didn't know you had guitar lessons with Mr Tingley!'

My sister's boyfriend Spike looks very, very scary, but actually, he is quite sweet. His real name is Sebastian Pike and he plays the cello.

He and Becca met in the school

orchestra and bonded over their love of backcombed hair and smudgy eyeliner.

'Yeah, Mr Tingley is cool,' Spike says gruffly. 'He's helping me explore my musical dark side.'

'Oh?'

'I'm in a band,' he explains. 'The Smashed Bananas. We're a thrash-metal-punk band. Our sound is all about chaos and destruction.'

'Oh,' I say again. 'That's . . . um . . . cool! I might start a band, once I can play a bit better.'

'Well, you don't actually *need* to be able to play guitar to be in a thrash-metal-punk band,' Spike explains. 'You just need a feeling for discord and disaster.'

'Oh,' I echo. I have never heard of thrash-metal-punk before, but it doesn't sound difficult exactly, if the racket coming from the studio a few minutes ago is anything to go by. As for the discord and disaster, I am surrounded by it. My life is one big disaster, pretty much.

Sounds like thrash-metal-punk could be perfect for me.

'We're going to enter the Battle of the Bands next month,' Spike says. 'Get some of your friends together and come and watch!'

'Maybe,' I sigh. 'If I am not in Malawi by then, tending to my herd of goats.'

Spike laughs. 'That won't happen,' he says.

'I hope not,' I tell him. 'Becca says that if Dad doesn't shut up about it, she will run off with you to join the circus.'

'Hmmm, she did mention something about learning to ride a unicycle,' Spike grins. 'But I wouldn't worry about it, Daizy. Really.'

'But Mum and Dad are arguing all the time,' I blurt. 'It's horrible. And Becca might run away and Pixie just wants a pet lion cub, and Jojo Tan-Sikorski got made Star of the Week at school for passing her Grade One piano exam. It's not fair. Nobody understands how I am feeling, nobody at all!'

Jojo Tan-Sikorski

Jojo Tan-Sikorski
GRADE ONE
PIANO EXAM

Spike sighs. 'It sounds pretty awful,' he says kindly. 'D'you know what I do when I'm feeling really fed up? I write about it. You know, songs and stuff. And I play my guitar and pour all my worries out into the music, and then it all feels better, somehow. You should try it.'

'I might,' I say.

I can't help thinking that Spike must have a lot of very worrying things on his mind, after listening to the racket he was making in Mr Tingley's studio. All the same, it could be a good idea.

'Anyway,' Spike says, 'come along to the Battle of the Bands, right? Bring some friends. And cheer up, Daizy – things are never as bad as you think.'

Actually, they may be worse, but I don't say that because Spike is only trying to be kind.

He hands me a leaflet, flicks back his green-tinted fringe and slopes off along the corridor.

'Daizy Star?' a voice calls out, and I wave at Spike's retreating back and walk into the studio.

Guitars and amps of all shapes and sizes are piled up in corners, and tangled loops of wire snake their way across the room. Piles of papers with mysterious-looking coded messages on them are scattered about on the lino floor.

Mr Tingley himself looks almost as old as my grandad, but he couldn't be more different. He has long dark hair, flecked with grey, parted in the middle and pulled back into a ponytail.

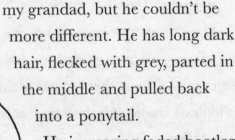

He is wearing faded bootleg jeans and tan-coloured cowboy boots and a faded T-shirt that says *Thin Lizzy*. It's probably some really ancient band because Mr Tingley is actually *not* very thin. And I really, really hope his first name isn't Lizzy.

'So, Daizy,' he says. 'You can call me Ted . . .'

Phew. I was worried there, for a moment.

'Your mum wants me to show you a few basic guitar chords,' he says. 'Well, you've come to the right place. I have worked with the stars. Ozzy Osbourne, Jimi Hendrix, Kurt Cobain . . .'

I have never heard of these people, but I am guessing they could be rock stars from way back in the mists of time because Ted Tingley is looking very proud. I try to look impressed.

'I'd like to be in a band too,' I tell him shyly. 'Maybe. One day.'

'Ah!' he grins. 'Interesting. What kind of a band?'

The kind of band that includes Beth, Willow and Murphy, really. I haven't got much further than that in my daydreams, although I want it to be cool and quirky and sell shedloads of CDs, obviously. Something like Miley Cyrus crossed with Pink and Taylor Swift, only without the cheesy American accents.

'A thrash-metal-punk band,' I say, then close my mouth fast before anything else scary and insane can leak out. Where did that come from? Like I said, disaster follows me like my own personal raincloud.

But Ted Tingley looks pleased.

'As I thought!' he declares. 'You are not the average eleven-year-old girl! You are different . . . daring . . . a girl with big dreams!'

'I am!' I agree. 'Very big dreams! I am looking for my star quality, and I thought . . . well, I wondered . . . if it might be playing the guitar?'

Ted Tingley narrows his eyes. 'Trust me,' he says. 'If you have star quality, I will find it!'

Looks like I came to the right place after all.

An hour later, I am not so sure. I have learnt my first guitar tune – well, almost. I am not quite perfect yet. 'Twinkle, Twinkle, Little Star' is actually a lot more complicated than you might think.

Ted Tingley is not looking quite as pleased as he was to begin with. His face has taken on a slightly pained expression, and he keeps checking his watch. I am not taking this personally, of course. Perhaps Ted has an important appointment with an ageing rock star, or a nettle and kidney-bean casserole in the oven.

I hope that's it, anyway.

'OK, OK, that's enough for today,' he says, even though we still have ten minutes of lesson time left. 'That was . . . really very interesting. Unexpected. Keep on practising, Daizy. I will teach you the chords for "Baa Baa Black Sheep", next week. And don't worry, everyone struggles a bit to start with.'

'Do you think I have talent?' I ask him eagerly.

Ted Tingley looks shifty, and he can't quite meet my eye. My heart sinks, but his words are surprisingly hopeful.

'Um . . . well . . . yes, of course you have talent, Daizy,' he says. 'Absolutely. Hidden talent,

maybe. Very, very hidden. Untapped as yet . . .
but never fear, I can uncover it. And you may be
right about the thrash-metal-punk idea because
you do seem to have a very special skill for chaos
and discord.'

'I do?' I grin.

'You do,' Ted Tingley insists. 'I have never
heard quite so much chaos from a beginner in all
my years as a guitar guru.'

I knew it. I just knew it! I can't stop smiling all
the way home. I have begun to uncover my star
quality and made a start on my rock princess
career. It is very exciting.

There's a cold breeze blowing. I push my
hands into my pockets and my
fingers curl round a crumpled
slip of paper. I pull
out the leaflet for
Spike's Battle of the
Bands competition and
scan it carelessly.

> **♫♫ WANTED! ♫♫**
>
> Young bands, new talent, rising
> ☆ stars! ☆
>
> ## The Battle of the Bands
>
> Brightford Playhouse
>
> 15th December
>
> 7–10 pm.
>
> win £500!!!

I read the leaflet once, twice, three times. Young bands. New talent. Rising stars . . . and £500!

With £500, you could do a lot. You could hire a pink limo and ride around town with your friends, or buy an Xbox or go on holiday to Disneyland. You could splash out on new clothes and funky haircuts and designer shoes, and watch

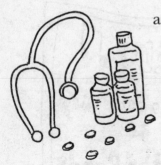

a new DVD every day.

Or you could dig a well, kit out a clinic with medicine, buy school books . . . and probably a whole herd of goats as well. £500 could go a long, long way in a village in Malawi.

And maybe then Dad wouldn't feel like he had to fix all the worries of the world himself. We wouldn't have to go and live in Malawi, and Mum would stop being all frowny and cross, and

Becca's life would not be ruined and Pixie could just look after her one existing pet, Nigel, the speckled newt Spike gave her for her birthday,

instead of dreaming of lion cubs and pet giraffes and tame antelopes. As for me, I wouldn't have to leave my school, my friends or my star

quality behind, just as I've finally found it.

£500 might just be the answer to all my problems. I am young, I have talent, and I might even be a rising star. I just need to get Beth, Willow and Murphy on board.

Battle of the Bands, here we come . . .

8

The next day at school, Ethan Miller hands me a plastic carrier bag containing a battered old football, a pair of studded boots and two of his old Man U footy kits. 'For the kids in Malawi,' he says with a grin, and legs it off into the middle of the nearest footy game.

Beth and Willow sigh. 'He's so kind!' Beth breathes. 'So caring!'

'So thoughtful,' Willow agrees. 'He's just . . . dreamy!'

'No, he's not!' I scowl. 'He's annoying. I *told*

him the kids in Malawi had better things to do than worry about football! Honestly!'

'He's only trying to help!' Murphy says, and I guess he has a point.

'You should be grateful!' Beth retorts.

But it's very hard to be grateful to a boy like Ethan Miller. I suppose that handing me the footy stuff was quite a kind thing to do, if misguided, but now I will have to lug his bag of tatty old footy kit around with me for the rest of the day. I mean, eewww. I hope he washed it first.

'Forget Ethan,' I tell my friends boldly. 'I have had a brilliant idea. We are going to win the Battle of the Bands!'

I show Beth, Willow and Murphy the crumpled leaflet and explain about the guitar lessons, and how Ted Tingley thinks I have hidden talents. 'All we need is a band,' I explain. 'Then we can win the five hundred pounds and send it to Malawi. Job done!'

'It might not be as simple as that,' Murphy frowns.

'Why not?' I ask. 'I need to do something. I can't rely on Mum to talk Dad out of this . . . lately, all they do is argue. It's horrible. If we can provide the money to get a village up on its feet, with medicines and goats and maths books and stuff . . . well, there'd be no need for any of us to actually go and live there! And then there'd be no more arguments, and everything would be fine again.'

Willow looks doubtful. 'I'm not sure that even five hundred pounds can do all that,' she says.

Beth nods. 'I think your dad likes the idea of going out there to actually help too,' she reminds me. 'You know . . . building a school, digging a well, that kind of thing. Would it make any difference?'

This isn't quite going how I planned. I decide on a different approach.

'We might even get to be famous,' I say.

Murphy raises an eyebrow, and Beth and Willow perk up at once.

'You think so?'

'I know so! Our CDs could go to number one! There would be posters of us on bedroom walls throughout the land! We could be the youngest rock stars ever!'

'Don't you think we might be a bit *too* young?' Willow asks.

'Of course not!' I tell her briskly. 'Age doesn't matter if you have what it takes!'

'Er, Daizy?' Murphy says. 'We can't actually play any instruments.'

'So what?' I huff.

I am a little bit disappointed, I admit. I am offering my friends a chance of fame and fortune, and all they can think of are little details like whether they can play an instrument or not. After all, Spike was very clear that you don't really need to be able to play your instruments if you're in a thrash-metal-punk band.

I wish Beth, Willow and Murphy would trust me. I have a plan that will save me from a life in the blistering African sun, stop my parents divorcing and shoot me and possibly my best friends to stardom at the same time. You'd think they would get a little bit more excited about it.

'Willow can sing,' I point out. 'And I will soon be an expert on my pink guitar. One of you can play bass, and one of you can be the drummer.'

'But . . .'

'Please?' I ask, as the bell rings for class. 'For me?'

'OK, OK,' Murphy sighs. 'For Malawi.'

'For a peaceful life,' Beth adds.

'For fame and fortune,' Willow grins. 'We'll do it!'

Miss Moon starts the day off with a random geography test. She warned us, and gave us an illustrated atlas to flick through at home, but I kind of forgot, what with the excitement of discovering my hidden talent and planning the band.

I will have to hope for the best.

Miss Moon goes around the class with a big straw hat filled with folded papers, like little raffle tickets. You have to pick out a paper, and on the paper is the name of a country, and you have to stand up and tell the class something about that country.

Murphy gets Italy, and he tells everybody that the capital is Rome and the national dish is pasta and that Italian ice cream is the best in the whole world. Beth gets

Japan, and she tells us that the capital is Tokyo and that they have cherry blossom and kimonos and make a fortune from

things like flat-screen TVs and motorbikes and chopsticks. Willow gets India, and although she gets the capital city wrong (she says it's Bombay, not Delhi) she does tell us that tea is

grown there, and that lots of people don't eat meat, and that one of their gods is a blue elephant with a very cool flowery necklace, which is all news to me.

Ethan Miller gets France, and he smirks and tells us that the capital is Paris and that the French liked to cut rich people's heads off, and that they eat things like snails and frogs' legs and horsemeat. I am certain this is a lie because who would do that? But it turns out that he is actually right, and I can't help thinking it is exactly the kind of revolting detail Ethan would know. Yuck.

Then it is my turn. I stick my hand into the hat and pull out a bit of paper, and open it. Peru, it says. I don't know anything at all about Peru. Not one single thing. Why did I have to pick Peru when other people got regular places like Italy and Japan and India and France?

I open my mouth and close it again, a little like a goldfish.

'Daizy?' Miss Moon says gently. 'Which country did you pick?'

I scrunch the paper up and hide it inside my fist. 'Malawi,' I announce. 'Malawi is in Africa. The capital city is Lilongwe. The people speak English and Chichewa. They grow tea, coffee, sugar and tobacco to export, and millet, rice, bananas and vegetables to eat. There are not enough schools or books, and there is not enough medicine, either. They have mosquitoes that give you a disease called malaria, and lots of children die of it every day. And that's crazy because nobody should get malaria at all. If everyone had a mosquito net to sleep under, it wouldn't be a problem, but hardly anyone has got one, and they only cost a pound! But I suppose it is hard to find a spare pound when you don't even have enough food to go round. And many places have no clean water and no doctors or nurses or teachers and, really, we don't know how lucky we are because we have so much and we take it all for granted. If you know what I mean.'

I sit down, my cheeks pink.

'Um . . . very good, Daizy,' Miss Moon says, looking a little stunned. 'Hmmm. I didn't even know that Malawi was in the hat . . . but well done, Daizy. You certainly know a lot about the place.'

What Miss Moon doesn't realize, is that it is possible I may know even more about Malawi before very much longer, but I can't bring myself to say this out loud. Maybe I'll just send the class a postcard:

Dear Year Six
Having fun in a tin hut on the Shores of Lake Malawi. Wish you were here, or I wasn't.
Lots of love,
Daizy Star xxx

Class Six
Stella Street Primary
Stella Street
Brightford
U.K.

MALAWI

Ethan Miller puts his hand up.

'Yes, Ethan?'

'They don't even have football there,' he says in outraged tones. 'It's not fair.'

'You're quite right, Ethan,' Miss Moon says. 'It isn't.'

'We should do something,' he says. 'Raise

money, collect old pairs of football boots, herds of goats, anything!'

'It's not so much about raising money as raising awareness,' Miss Moon frowns. 'Helping the Malawi people to be independent and self-sufficient. We have as much to learn from them as they have to learn from us. But you are right, Ethan; perhaps there is something we can do . . . I'll think about it.'

Beth elbows me in the ribs. 'See?' she whispers. 'He's my hero!'

I wouldn't go that far, but maybe, just maybe, Ethan Miller is not a complete loser. Just a partial one.

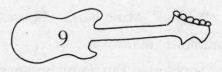

9

When Pixie and I get home from school, the house is in uproar. Mum, still in her nurse's uniform, is yelling at Dad, who is trying to show her some glossy leaflets about voluntary work in Malawi.

'You said we needed to do more research,' Dad says. 'And I agreed. It's all arranged. I have signed up for a three-week stint with a project in northern Malawi . . . just me. They needed someone fast because one of their volunteers has just dropped out. The flights were booked already, and they changed the details this afternoon so I can use the tickets. It's perfect!'

'You're going to Malawi?' Mum asks icily.
She is not yelling now, and that's scarier,
somehow. 'Alone?'

'I thought you'd be pleased!'

'Pleased?' Mum barks. '*Pleased?* Mike, are you
completely mad?'

Dad blinks. 'But it's all organized now! It was
a great opportunity. I had to act quickly or I
might have missed it! I will be able to see what
the place is like, work out where we can live,
how we can fit in. I know you need a little more
time to come to terms with the idea, Livvi. This
will give you that time. I thought that's what you
wanted!'

'I want you to stop this stupid idea, Mike!'
Mum yells, and her eyes brim with tears. 'I do
not want you to go off on your own to the other
side of the world without us! It's . . . it's . . .
ridiculous!'

Then she catches sight of me, with Pixie
cowering behind. She slaps a hand over her
mouth.

'Oh, Daizy, Pixie,
I didn't see you there,'
she whispers. 'I'm sorry.'

My heart is
thumping, and there
is a sick, empty feeling in
my stomach that has
nothing to do
with hunger.

'Is Dad going to
Malawi?' I ask, and my voice
sounds wobbly, even to me.
'Without us?'

'Dad's leaving?' Pixie wails.

Dad scoops the two of us up in a big bear
hug.

'It's nothing to worry about,' he says. 'Yes, I
am going to Malawi, but just for three weeks, to
help with the project in Tatu Mtengo. We'll be
building a school and digging a well. I want to
see what it's really like out there, work out how
best we can help . . .'

'It's just for a little while,' Mum says, wiping her eyes. 'Nothing is settled yet. Your dad will be back before you know it.'

But this is not a holiday we are talking about, it's a trip to Africa. Without us. My stomach churns.

'When are you going, Dad?' I whisper.

'Not yet,' he says, trying to sound upbeat. 'Not for another week.'

And that's when I start to panic because this nightmare is happening. And it's happening now.

It goes from bad to worse. Becca gets home and tells Dad she's glad he's going.

'Go by yourself,' she tells him coldly. 'See if I care! I'm not coming, that's for sure. And besides, it might be a bit saner around this place without you!'

Dad looks dismayed, but what did he expect? That we'd be jumping for joy at the idea? He takes himself off for a run to escape the frosty atmosphere.

Becca, Pixie and Mum curl up on the sofa

with a huge bar of chocolate
and Pixie's *Little Mermaid* DVD.
We have all seen that film so
many times we know it off by
heart. Watching it again is like settling down and
wrapping yourself up in a soft, warm blanket –
comforting and familiar and somehow calming.
The chocolate helps too, but big, fat tears keep
rolling down Mum's cheeks, and Becca mutters
'*He is ruining my life!*' under her breath every now
and again. All in all, it's kind of depressing.

'Aren't you watching?' Pixie asks me, with a
quivering lip. 'It might be the last time we ever
see it!' I doubt that, somehow.

I would love to curl up, eat chocolate and
watch mermaids, lobsters and talking fish
frolicking about on film, but sadly, that won't
change anything. And I know something that
just might . . .

I call an emergency band meeting.

'What band?' Murphy has the cheek to say

when I phone him, but as soon as I tell him my
life is in tatters and my dad has booked his ticket
to Africa, he snaps to attention pretty quick.
Soon, he, Beth and Willow are holed up in my
bedroom.

'Things are desperate,' I tell them truthfully.
'We need to get this band idea moving – now.
It's the only thing that can save me! What if Dad
decides to stay in Malawi?' I wail. 'What if he
just rings and tells us to pack our bags and come
out to join him? It just feels so real now!'

'Doesn't sound as though your mum is too
keen,' Beth points out. 'She looked like she'd
been crying when she answered the door.'

'She had,' I say gloomily. 'Crying and yelling.
And the other night, she and Dad were arguing
until way past midnight. I don't know what feels
scarier – the idea of going to live in Malawi,
or . . . or . . .'

There is a lump in my throat the size of a
small grapefruit.

I can't say it, not out loud. I can't say that I'm

scared my mum and dad might split up over this.

Beth and Willow seem to sense my distress, though, because they each put an arm round me and hug me tight. By the time I pull away there is

a damp patch on Beth's shoulder, and Willow is holding my hand so tightly it hurts. It seems impossible that anything bad could happen to me when I have such cool friends, but something bad is happening. Something very, very bad. My dad is leaving us to live in sub-Saharan Africa. He couldn't get further away if he tried. And what if he doesn't come back? Last year, Kelly Munroe's dad ran off with the woman from the chip shop on the corner, but they only went as far as Bridge Street. At least Kelly gets to see her dad on weekends, and she gets free chips whenever she wants them.

I can't see myself nipping over to Tatu Mtengo for visits, or not very often, anyway. And I bet they don't have chips there.

Murphy takes a bag of custard doughnuts from under his jacket and offers me one. 'Good for pain,' he says wisely. 'And they taste better than medicine.'

He's right about that, of course.

'So,' I snuffle, in between mouthfuls, 'it's

serious. Winning the Battle of the Bands is my last hope. Dad should be home from Malawi by then, and if he sees us up on stage – sees how amazing we are – well, he'll come to his senses and realize he cannot take me away from all this. From my friends, my school, my star quality . . .'

'Custard doughnuts,' Murphy muses.

'Yes, them too,' I agree. 'He will see the error of his ways. He will be proud of me, and he will turn to Mum and look at her, and everything will go all mushy and kind of soft focus like it does in the films, and they will fall in love all over again.'

'I hope so,' Beth sighs.

'And then I will hand over our cheque for five hundred pounds, and we can really help the children of Tatu Mtengo, and all my troubles will be over!'

'Ri-ight,' Willow frowns. 'I hope so too.'

'What kind of a band did you say we were?' Murphy asks.

'Thrash-metal-punk,' I explain. 'Ted Tingley, my guitar guru, suggested it. And Spike. It is all about destruction and disaster and you don't even have to be any good at your instruments!'

'Well, that's *something*, I guess,' Beth frowns. 'But, Daizy . . . we don't actually have any instruments!'

'My dad has an old bass guitar in the attic,' Murphy offers. 'I'll dig it out.'

'Brilliant,' I grin. 'I've got the pink guitar, obviously, and we can practise with the school drum kit too. You could be the drummer, Beth, and Willow can sing!'

'We don't have any songs, either,' Willow argues.

'I'm on to it,' I tell them. 'I've been writing stuff myself. I have two songs already! "Malawi Madness" and "My Dad's Mid-life Crisis". What do you think?'

'They sound . . . interesting,' Willow says doubtfully.

Murphy sighs. 'I'm not really sure about this, Daizy Star,' he says. 'But if you think it will help, I'll give it a go.'

'We can do it!' I tell him. 'I know we can!'

'I'm in too,' Beth sighs. 'Does it have to be the drums, though? Couldn't I play the triangle or something?'

'They do not have triangle players in a thrash-metal-punk band,' I tell her firmly.

'I suppose I'm in too,' Willow shrugs. 'Who knows, it might even be fun!'

A thrash-metal-punk band is not supposed to be fun, of course, but I decide to keep quiet about that.

'That's settled then!' I grin. 'Thank you, Beth, Willow, Murphy. You are the best friends ever, in the whole entire universe.'

I fling my arms round them in a group hug. I knew they wouldn't let me down! We pull apart, laughing.

'What about a name for the band?' Murphy asks. 'How about The Custard Doughnuts?'

'The Pink Guitars?' Willow offers.

'I like it,' I say, 'but we need something dark and sinister. We are a thrash-metal-punk band, remember? How about The Mouldy Meatballs?'

'Or something really gross, like The Festering Scabs!' Beth chips in, and we all turn and look at her.

'What?' she says. 'I like it!'

'It might be a little bit *too* gross,' Willow says faintly.

We'll find a name, though. And we'll practise like crazy, and get really, really good. And then we will win the Battle of the Bands – and stop my family from falling apart. Sorted!

10

Our first practice is in the school music room at lunchtime next day. I have brought in my pink guitar, Murphy has his dad's old bass, and Beth settles herself nervously behind the school drum kit. Willow leafs through the lyrics for the songs I have written.

I plug in the pink guitar.

'I'll show you what I've worked out so far, tunes-wise, and you can just join in when you've got the idea!' I tell them.

'I'm not sure about this,' Beth says, hitting one of the cymbals half-heartedly with a drumstick.

But I am.

I crash into action, racking up the amp to full

blast and strumming the pink guitar until my fingers hurt. Nobody joins in with me, so I close my eyes and belt out the words to the song myself.

'My dad's mid-life crisis is tearing me to pieces,
I watch his happy face wrinkle up in little creases.
He is acting very strange and weird
And now the thing that I've most feared
Is happening, and happening fast . . .
How long can a mid-life crisis last?'

When I open my eyes after the last heart-rending line, Beth, Willow and Murphy are staring at me, open-mouthed. I expect they are amazed at how far I have come in such a short time on my journey to rock stardom.

'That's . . . that's . . . very unusual,' Willow says at last.

'You could sing it better,' I tell her generously. 'I am not a singer. I am more of a lead guitarist. Ted Tingley says I have hidden depths.'

My dad's midlife crisis is tearing me to pieces...

'I'm sure you do,' Murphy says kindly. 'But, Daizy, that tune . . . I'm not trying to be funny, but it sounded a bit like a mangled version of "Twinkle Twinkle Little Star"!'

'That's exactly what it's meant to be!' I tell him. 'Cool, huh?'

'It's just a little bit . . . weird,' Beth ventures.

'Messed up,' Willow says.

'I knew you'd like it!' I tell them. 'We are a thrash-metal-punk band, after all! And we need something that will make us stand out from the other bands. This is it! Nursery rhymes with a darker side! You have to kind of screech the words, Willow.'

'Ri-ight,' Willow says.

'And the rest of you, just make it up as you go along,' I say. 'Remember, it has to be loud and thrashy and dramatic.'

We start off slowly, which is to be expected. Murphy can't get the hang of the bass, and Beth is too nervous to really bash away at the drums. Gradually, though, we start to relax, and by the end of lunch break we are actually getting somewhere.

Willow is howling out the lyrics like a wolf in pain, Murphy is slamming away at the bass while Beth wallops the drum kit in a violent frenzy that is really quite impressive. The overall effect is so deafening that we don't notice right away when Mr Bleecher, the school janitor, bursts in, scowling and waving his mop around.

'Oi!' he yells as the last jangling chords of 'Malawi Madness' trail away. 'What do you kids think you're doing? Bloomin' vandals! This is school property you're wrecking! Get out of here!'

'We are having a band practice,' I say importantly. 'Miss Moon knows we're in here.'

'Everybody knows you're in here!' Mr Bleecher snorts. 'I could hear you all the way from the boiler room! My head is splitting!'

'We're just finishing now, Mr Bleecher,' Beth says. 'Sorry if we've given you a headache. Music is our new hobby. We're just learning. We need all the practice we can get.'

'We'll keep the sound turned down in future,' Murphy promises.

Mr Bleecher scowls and shuffles off, still muttering.

'Oh dear,' Beth says. 'I don't think he liked it.'

I grin. 'A thrash-metal-punk band is always misunderstood by adults,' I explain. 'They are too set in their ways to understand.'

'So . . . you actually think that practice was OK?' Willow checks. 'You think we might be in with a chance?'

'A chance?' I echo. 'We are in with more than just a chance. What does Mr Bleecher know?

98

We're bound to be a bit wobbly to start with, but just you wait. By the time the Battle of the Bands rolls around, we'll be better. We'll blow their socks off!'

Murphy is over at my place, showing me some sketches he's made. He is trying to come up with a band image for us, so we can look really cool (as well as sounding it) at the Battle of the Bands. We are in Becca's room because she is our resident expert on thrash-metal-punk music, and partly because she has the secret stash of hot chocolate and marshmallows. Pixie is in here too, taking refuge because Mum and Dad are arguing again – this time about whether Dad needs a new sunhat for Malawi.

Our house is like a war zone lately.

'I like this one,' I tell Murphy, pointing to a sketch where Beth, Willow and me are wearing outsize black T-shirts splattered with random blotches of bright paint. The T-shirts are gathered on the hips with studded belts, worn

like mini-dresses with stripy socks and clumpy
boots. Murphy, as the only boy in the band, gets
to wear red skinny jeans and a smaller version of
the paint-splattered T-shirt.

'I like it too,' Becca nods. 'You, Willow and
Beth could crimp and backcomb your hair and
tie scarves and ribbons into it. I can lend you my

pink eyeshadow and my black lipstick too.'

'Thanks,' I say, trying hard to look as though I mean it. 'We have an image, we have songs . . . now we just need a name.'

It is not easy to find a name for a thrash-metal-punk band – seriously. You need a name that is edgy. I think of Spike's band, The Smashed Bananas. Maybe it just needs to be weird?

'Something inspired by Africa, maybe?' Murphy asks. 'Like . . . I dunno, Lion Attack?'

'I might be getting a lion cub,' Pixie muses. 'When we live in Malawi. I haven't decided yet. I fancied a giraffe, but I think I have changed my mind. You'd need a really, really tall kennel to keep it in.'

'A giraffe is not like a dog,' Becca points out. 'You can't keep one in a kennel.'

'Well, anyway, I don't want one any more,' Pixie says.

'The Jilted Giraffes!' Becca giggles.

'The Wayward Wildebeests!' Murphy suggests.

I don't think they are taking this seriously at all.

'I think that what I would really, really, *really* like when we get to Malawi is actually a honey badger,' Pixie declares.

Everyone looks at Pixie.

'A honey badger?' I echo. 'I've never heard of a honey badger!'

Becca smirks. 'That's because there is no such thing,' she says. 'Pixie, you can't just invent random animals. And anyway, we are NOT going to Malawi. I've already told you, I will pack my bags and run away with Spike to join the circus if Dad tries to make me go.'

'There is *too* such a thing as a honey badger!' Pixie says plaintively. 'They are the most fearless animal in all of Africa!'

'Pixie!' Becca says sharply. 'Don't make up stories! Honestly!'

My little sister has a very vivid imagination.

'They are real!' Pixie is protesting. 'They're in a book at school! And I looked them up on the Internet – so there. I can PROVE it! Just wait there – I'll get Dad's computer!'

And three minutes later, we are huddled round Dad's laptop, looking at pictures of funny little black and white creatures – different to British badgers, but still pretty cool. They love to eat honey. And sure enough, for their size, they are just about the bravest, fiercest animals ever.

'See?' Pixie says.

'Right,' Becca says. 'I mean, I wasn't saying they didn't exist, I was just saying . . .' She smiles sheepishly. 'Sorry, Pixie.'

'They look kind of Goth-like,' Murphy says. 'Cute, but ferocious.'

'The Honey Badgers,' I say thoughtfully. '*THE HONEY BADGERS!*'

I will have to check it with Beth and Willow, of course, but I think we've found a name for the band!

11

D ad is packing his suitcase for Malawi. He
puts in lots of shirts with short sleeves and
hideous flowery patterns, those awful shorts he
wore in Eastbourne in the summer and a pair of
big flat leather sandals that show his pale, hairy
toes. There is a floppy straw hat too, slightly
frayed round the edges because
Dad said there is no
point in investing in
a new sunhat when
the old one is
perfectly good.
Perfectly hideous,
more like.

My dad is going to look like a madman when he gets to Malawi.

'I'll miss you!' I tell him. 'Do you *have* to go?'

Dad looks serious. 'It's been a dream of mine ever since I was a student, Daizy,' he says. 'I want to travel, but it's more than that – I want to give something back, make a difference.'

'I wish you could just make a difference from here,' I sigh. 'I do understand why you want to help . . . I do too. I've sorted out some of my best books for you to take over. You said the kids out there don't have very much.'

Dad's face lights up.

'Daizy, that's wonderful!' he says. 'These will be so welcome!'

'There's this old football and some kit and boots to go with it,' I add, handing over Ethan Miller's offering. 'This yucky boy at school brought them in for you to take.'

Then Pixie hands over an old rag doll and Becca donates a pair of pink fingerless gloves, and Dad smiles and says he is proud to have such thoughtful, generous daughters.

'You will come back, won't you?' I ask.

'Daizy!' Dad exclaims. 'Of course I will! I want us all to be together – you know that!'

The trouble is, Dad wants us all to be together in *Malawi*, and everyone else wants us all to be together here.

At least I hope everyone else wants us all to be together. Mum is still tight-lipped and quiet. There have been no more big rows, but I can tell she is not happy about any of this. Maybe she is actually quite glad to be shot of Dad for a while?

'What if you *don't* come back, though?' Pixie pipes up anxiously. 'What if you get eaten by a leopard or savaged by a ferocious honey badger?'

'What if you get malaria?' I chip in. 'Or typhoid fever?'

'Not going to happen,' Dad sighs. 'Don't worry, girls, I'll be fine!'

'Better take some suncream,' Mum says crisply. 'You know how you turn beetroot in the sun and peel like a sheet of flaky pastry.'

Dad huffs. 'I have done my research, thank you, Livvi,' he says curtly. 'It is actually the rainy season in Malawi right now. I shall be packing an umbrella, not suncream, thank you very much.'

'Don't say I didn't warn you,' Mum snaps.

If only we could go back to how life was before Dad packed his job in and got a mid-life crisis. I don't like the way things are now, not one little bit.

We go to the airport to say goodbye, of course. We line up in the check-in hall while Dad books in his suitcase and then we have milkshakes and muffins in one of the cafes, and even Dad has a strawberry smoothie and a triple choc chip muffin because muffins are probably very rare indeed in Malawi and he may not get the chance to taste one again for quite a while.

Then we trail along to customs, and that is where we have to say goodbye. It's kind of upsetting. Pixie starts sobbing and begging Dad not to get himself trampled by a herd of hippos, and I fling my arms round his neck and hang on so tightly I don't think I will ever let go. Even

Becca hugs Dad quickly and tells him things won't be the same without him.

Well, they won't. Who will make us beansprout crumble and fig and beetroot upside-down cake now that Dad is going away?

Hmm – no more disgustingly healthy dinners! I suppose every cloud has a silver lining.

'Well, then,' Mum says gruffly. 'Take care, Mike. Keep in touch.'

Dad just nods and turns towards customs, but right at the last minute he turns back and lifts Mum up in a big bear hug. When they finally pull apart, I notice that Mum is dabbing at her eyes, which has to be a good sign, surely?

It means she's going to miss him.

And then he's gone, stepping through the

magnetic archway and being frisked by
uniformed guards before disappearing towards
the departure lounge.

'Oh, Mike,' Mum whispers. 'You silly, silly
man.'

We head for home.

12

The house seems all wrong without Dad. There are no more rows about whether we should watch a wildlife programme instead of *The Simpsons*. There are no more disgusting cabbage soup aromas, or misshapen home-made bread made with nuts and seeds you could just about break a tooth on. We go back to fish fingers and mash, or cheesy baked beans on toast, or pizza and oven chips with spaghetti hoops.

I'm almost missing tofu and beansprouts – seriously.

Nobody remembers to take the rubbish out on dustbin day, and nobody does the washing-up,

and the dirty dishes pile up in the sink. Both of
those things were Dad's jobs, and he isn't here to
do them. Pixie and me wash up in the end, but
Pixie drops a plate and Mum snaps at her to be
more careful. Pixie's eyes brim with tears.

'I'm sorry, Pixie,' she says, sighing. 'I know you
didn't mean it. I'm just so tired and so . . . well,
I don't know. Out of sorts, I suppose.'

'Are you worrying about Dad?' I ask.

'Why would I worry about your dad?' Mum
sighs. 'Swanning off to Africa like that . . .
ridiculous! The man has taken leave of his
senses!'

I kind of agree, but it makes me feel all churny and sad inside to hear Mum saying it out loud. Dad is thousands of miles away in the blistering heat of Malawi, but Mum is still angry with him.

Oh dear.

Dad phones on Sunday from his mobile, after a bumpy, twelve-hour jeep journey from the airport that finally took him to the village of Tatu Mtengo.

'It means Three Trees,' he tells us, sounding faraway and slightly echoey. 'It is very beautiful. I can see why Malawi is called the warm heart of Africa. The people have made me very welcome. They loved the books, Daizy, and the rag doll, and the pink gloves. And there is a whole team of boys charging around with the football right now. They are over the moon!'

I frown. Who knew that boys are just as crazy about kicking a football around in Malawi as they are here? The world is probably full of boys like Ethan Miller. Now that is a scary thought.

On Monday, Dad calls again.

'I have been eating *nsima*,' he tells us. 'It's like a white cornmeal porridge, like thin mashed potatoes. Yesterday, I ate it with monkey nuts. Today I ate it with mustard leaves. Tomorrow, I think someone mentioned *nsima* with deep-fried mice –'

'Don't!' I screech down the phone at him. 'Please, *please* don't eat mouse porridge! Say you are vegetarian!'

'It's a delicacy,' Dad replies. 'I don't want to offend anyone!'

'You're offending me!' I wail, but Dad just laughs.

He tells Mum he is staying with a couple called Hope and Andrew Nungu and their five children. The house is made of mud bricks with a thatched roof, but there is no running water or electricity in the whole village. Work has begun on digging the well, and some of the volunteers are beginning on the school building too.

'Have you found me a pet honey badger yet?'

Pixie wants to know, but Dad said he hasn't seen anything but chickens and goats in the village of Tatu Mtengo.

On Tuesday, Dad rings to say that he managed to avoid the deep-fried mice and stuck to fried cassava instead. Malawi is very, very hot, even though it seems to rain every single day in a tropical-storm kind of a way. Dad says he wishes he had listened to Mum and taken the suntan cream because his nose is getting burnt.

'Told you so,' Mum says.

Dad is missing us, he says.

'We miss you too!' I snuffle. 'You have to phone every single day. Promise?'

'I promise,' Dad replies. 'I'll have my mobile, even if I can't get to a regular phone.'

'I painted a picture of you today in art!' Pixie chips in. 'You were digging the well and a whole herd of zebras had gathered round to watch you!'

'Lovely!' Dad says. He explains that he hasn't seen any zebra yet, but that there has been a

Monkey Alert that day. A pack of monkeys descended on the village of Tatu Mtengo, and children ran out to chase them away.

'Maybe a pet monkey would be cool?' Pixie considers.

Becca just rolls her eyes, and Mum shakes her head, and I can see that neither of them is impressed with the idea of living in a place where monkey raids are an everyday hazard.

I guess I'm not, either.

On Wednesday, there is no phone call at all.

'He promised!' I say. 'He said he'd ring!'

'Maybe he ate the deep-fried mice and he's too scared to tell us?' Pixie wonders.

'Perhaps his mobile is out of battery,' Mum sighs. 'After all, there is no electricity in the village. He won't be able to charge it up. I hope he remembered to take spares . . .'

We look at each other. Dad packed dodgy sandals, flowery shirts, a sunhat, a Frisbee, malaria tablets. None of us remembers seeing spare batteries.

'Perhaps he'll write?' I say hopefully.

'I'm sure I remember him saying that the postal service is almost non-existent in rural

Malawi,' Mum frowns.

Just when you think things cannot get any worse, they do. My dad is stuck in far-flung Malawi with no working mobile phone, no email and no postal service. Anything could happen.

He might choke on a deep-fried mouse, or get some tropical illness, or fall into the well he is digging and drown. Or he might just forget all about us. I'm not sure which would be worse.

'Are we a one-parent family now?' Pixie asks on Dad's tenth day in Tatu Mtengo, right in the middle of watching *Scooby-Doo*. 'Do we have a broken home?'

I just about drop the remote control.

'No!' I tell her, shocked. 'Where did you get that idea?'

Pixie sighs. 'I told Amelia Hutchins my dad had gone to Africa to find me a pet honey badger,' she explains. 'Amelia said that her dad went out last Easter to get a pint of milk and never came back. He ran away to Blackpool and ended up working on the Pleasure Beach.'

'You're joking, right?'

'No,' Pixie says. 'Amelia's mum and dad got divorced, and now she has a broken home.'

I blink. What is it with middle-aged dads? First it was Kelly's dad and the girl from the chip shop, and now Amelia's dad and the pint of milk. It's a very flimsy excuse for a divorce, if you ask me. Maybe the local shop had run out of milk, but all the same, I can't believe anyone would go all the way to Blackpool Pleasure Beach just for a pint of semi-skimmed.

It is starting to look as though middle-aged dads can't be trusted.

'Mum and Dad are *not* getting a divorce,' I declare, sounding much more confident than I feel. 'No way. Dad is doing voluntary work in Malawi and following his dream. That's all.'

'He's getting me a honey badger too,' Pixie adds.

'Well, maybe.'

'Definitely,' Pixie says, turning back to *Scooby-*

Doo. 'I knew Amelia was wrong. I told her that our home is not broken at all, except for the kitchen cupboard door, and the bottom shelf in the fridge.'

I'm not sure that's quite what Amelia meant, but I don't argue.

Perhaps at the moment, technically, we are a single-parent family, but that is only because Dad is working abroad for three weeks. He will be back soon and everything will go back to normal.

I hope.

13

School is just about the only thing that keeps me sane, but it is not easy to care very much about long division and spelling tests when everything else is falling to bits. And no, I am not talking about the kitchen cupboard door.

Miss Moon calls me over to her desk one lunchtime as everyone else is filing out towards the canteen.

'Daizy,' she says, her green eyes sparkly and kind, 'is there anything worrying you?'

I blink.

Where do I start? I am worried because Dad has been gone for thirteen days now, and we haven't heard from him for well over a week.

I am worried he has forgotten us, or fallen down the well he is digging and drowned. I am worried he has been killed by a python or trampled by an elephant or stung by a deadly mosquito. Even now, he could be lying in a hut made from dusty red bricks, burning up with a fever, delirious, dying. It could happen. He could die without ever knowing that I have discovered my star quality.

'Why do you ask?' I say, stalling for time.

Miss Moon opens my English jotter. Earlier on, we were asked to write a poem about how we were feeling today. Maybe I was a bit too honest?

Sick And Tired

I'm sick and tired of French and maths,
Sick and tired of playground laughs,
I'm sick and tired of science and art,
Cos my whole life is falling apart.
In Malawi life is tough,
Life is hard and life is rough.
A mosquito with a nasty bite
Might come and get you in the night,

And then you will be really sick,
No medicine to do the trick.
I'm sick and tired of all the lies,
Sick and tired of hungry cries.
Sometimes it's too hard to bear,
Why can life be so UNFAIR?

Miss Moon looks at me, obviously concerned. 'This isn't the first time you've mentioned Malawi at school,' she says. 'You haven't been your usual bouncy self just lately, Daizy Star. And then there are the band practices. I can't help noticing it all sounds very . . . um . . . loud and . . . well, angry.'

'Has Mr Bleecher been complaining?' I ask.

'Not just Mr Bleecher,' Miss Moon admits. 'Several of the teachers have commented. I am all for you and your friends practising your music, Daizy, but as your teacher I am just a little bit concerned.'

'Are you going to stop us from practising?' I ask, alarmed.

'No, no, of course not!' she says. 'I have defended you in the staffroom. This band is obviously very important to you.'

'It is! And besides, we are a thrash-metal-punk band. We are supposed to sound loud and angry!'

'I see,' she sighs. 'But, Daizy . . . I have to ask . . . is something on your mind?'

So many things are on my mind, it's like wearing a concrete sunhat. It weighs me down . . . and it seems to get heavier every day.

I bite my lip. 'I just don't see why we should have so much when the people in Malawi have so little!' I blurt out. 'It's not fair!'

'No, it isn't,' Miss Moon agrees. 'You're right. Life can be very unfair indeed.'

'I think about it all the time,' I admit. 'It makes me sad. And angry.'

'I can see that,' Miss Moon nods. 'But . . . there is a lot of poverty and hardship in the world. Why are you worrying about Malawi in particular?'

125

I sigh. 'My dad has gone to do some voluntary work there,' I explain. 'He is digging a well and helping to build a school for a village called Tatu Mtengo. He's been gone for thirteen whole days, and we haven't heard anything since last Tuesday! It's very worrying! What if something has happened to him?'

'I'm sure he's fine,' Miss Moon says kindly. 'It's probably very difficult to communicate from somewhere like Malawi, but if anything were wrong, you'd know. But of course, I can see that the band is clearly helping you to express your mixed-up feelings about it all.'

'It's not just that, Miss,' I confide. 'We are entering the Battle of the Bands, and we are going to win. We have to, because the prize is five hundred pounds and that money could buy a herd of goats and build a new clinic and supply school books and medicine for a place like Tatu Mtengo!'

Miss Moon looks doubtful. 'I see,' she says, but I'm not sure she can really see at all, and that makes me sad.

'Daizy . . .' Miss Moon says, as I turn to go. 'Don't be too disappointed if you don't win the Battle of the Bands. I know you have been practising hard, and I know how much it means to you, but . . . well, some bands try for years and years before they manage to break through to the big time. I don't want you to be disappointed, that's all.'

I won't be disappointed, of course, because losing is not an option. The Honey Badgers are going to win . . . and my dad will come home safely and remember that he loves me, Becca, Pixie and Mum far too much to be separated from us ever again. He will not be tempted to run off with anybody from the chip shop, or get huffy because the shop has run out of milk and demand an instant divorce.

No way.

The forms have been filled in and sent away. The songs have been polished, the set has

been practised until it is just
about perfect. Mr Bleecher
has taken to wearing
earmuffs for the whole of the
lunch hour, and muttering
darkly whenever he sees us.

Ted Tingley, my guitar guru,
says I am a remarkable student. He says I am
breaking down walls and barriers, taking thrash-
metal-punk guitar to frightening new heights. Or
maybe it was depths, I can't remember.

'I have never had a pupil quite like you, Daizy
Star,' he says. He says it every week, and he
shakes his head sadly. I expect he is remembering
his own youth and wishing he'd had the ability
to turn 'Mary Had a Little Lamb' into a thrash-
metal-punk classic.

'Are you sure about this, Daizy?' he asked,
when I told him I'd posted off The Honey
Badgers' entry for the Battle of the Bands. 'Are
you sure the world is ready for your . . . um . . .
unique guitar style?'

I am not sure, but I hope the world is ready. They have to be, really, because I have something to say and let's face it, the world needs to hear it. And if they don't hear that message when Willow is yelling it out at 3,000 decibels over the sound of mangled guitar bass and drums, then they will never, ever hear it.

We are going to turn our amps up to the max. We are going to put our hearts and souls into the performance, and also our blood, our sweat and our tears.

We are going to win the Battle of the Bands, and the £500, and if we are lucky, one of Miss Moon's Star of the Week awards each as well.

Why not?

After all, this week Andy Hines got a Star of the Week award for having his tonsils out. And he got ice cream and jelly after the operation too.

Spike brought us some posters for the Battle of the Bands, and we have pinned them up at school. Beth has used her special calligraphy skills to write out invites for our parents and friends. There is an invite for Miss Moon and, unfortunately, one for Ethan Miller too.

'Why?' I huff. 'Why ask him? He is just not a thrash-metal-punk kind of boy. He wouldn't come, anyway.'

'He might,' Beth shrugs. 'And besides, I am not really a thrash-metal-punk kind of girl. I think Ethan would come and see us. He's really sensitive.'

I choke on my strawberry smoothie. Trust me, Ethan Miller is about as sensitive as a herd of rhinos, only not quite as good looking.

'He did give you that football for Malawi,' Willow chips in. 'He's very caring.'

'Very annoying, more like,' I frown. 'Still, I suppose it won't hurt to give him an invite. It's not like he'll actually turn up.'

'He might,' Beth says dreamily. 'To see

me play the drums!'

'To hear me sing,' Willow corrects her. 'To see me in the spotlight, lead singer of a thrash-metal-punk band!'

I narrow my eyes. It occurs to me that Beth and Willow may not be taking The Honey Badgers as seriously as I'd like. For them, the band may not be a matter of life or death, more a matter of getting Ethan's attention.

Still, if it keeps my friends keen, I suppose it is OK.

They give Ethan an invite, and he grins and says he will definitely be there. Miss Moon promises to come along, and Ted Tingley says he wouldn't miss my debut for the world, and besides, as an internationally famous guitar guru, he is on the panel of judges.

'You're a judge?' I ask him, wide-eyed.

'Well . . . yes!' he admits. 'Like I just said!'

It has to be a sign. My very own guitar guru will be helping to choose the winners. I already know how much Ted Tingley loves my music. He

has taught me everything I know. The Honey Badgers may still be a little rough around the edges, but surely, with Ted on our side, we cannot fail?

'You must be fair about it,' I tell him. 'Give the other bands a chance.'

Ted Tingley gives me a funny look. 'Er . . . right,' he says, looking shifty. I expect he won't be able to help himself.

And now the costumes are almost done.

I have fabric paint in my hair, fabric paint on my nose and chin, fabric paint on my shoes and all over my art shirt. Luckily, some of it actually made it on to the T-shirts too. They look seriously cool.

Murphy decided that flicking

the paint on instead of using a brush was the best
idea to get a totally random and chaotic effect.
It's a good job we covered the kitchen table with
newspaper first, and covered up our clothes with
our school art shirts. You can get kind of carried
away designing thrash-metal-punk T-shirts.

Willow has been making black fur-fabric ears
attached to headbands, to give us that edgy
honey-badger look, and Becca has tested out a
few weird Goth hairdos and make-up looks on
us. We are cool, we are sussed, we are
ready to win the Battle of the Bands.

At least, I hope we are.

We hang the finished T-shirts over
the clothes rack to dry, clear up the
newspaper and wash the brushes.

'Feeling OK?' Murphy checks.

'Feeling great!' I tell him. 'One more
practice at school tomorrow, then it's

really happening. At last! The Battle of the Bands! Fame and fortune are at our feet. And all our troubles will be over!'

Murphy frowns. 'I hope so,' he says.

'I *know* so,' I grin. 'Dad will be back from Malawi tomorrow. We still haven't heard from him, but Mum rang the charity a few days ago, and they said everything is fine. He just can't call from where he is now, that's all. He will be on the plane home tomorrow morning, as planned . . . Mum's taking the day off work to meet him at the airport. Boy, will he be surprised when he finds out about The Honey Badgers!'

'Yeah . . .' Murphy says.

'And then, when we win . . .'

Murphy rakes a hand through his long fringe and fixes me with a serious look. 'Daizy,' he says carefully, 'have you thought about what might happen if we *don't* win?'

I blink. Not win? But we *have* to win, Murphy knows that. Without that prize money, we are lost. This is not just about mosquito nets and medicine and school books. It's about stopping my family from falling apart.

'Of course we'll win,' I shrug. 'Obviously. We have worked so hard! We've practised every day! We have original material, a unique style and a sound that could turn the rock world upside down, everybody says so!'

'Daizy . . .' Murphy looks troubled. 'Not everybody says so. What about Mr Bleecher and his earmuffs?'

'Mr Bleecher is ancient!' I argue. 'What would he know about music? He probably listens to Cliff Richard! We are breaking down barriers, pushing the boundaries –'

'But . . . those other bands might be doing that too!' Murphy protests. 'They might be brilliant! And all of them will be older than us. What about Spike's band, The Smashed Bananas?

135

They play gigs and everything. They even got a CD played on Radio Basingstoke last week. They might be quite hard to beat!'

Radio Basingstoke? Becca must have kept pretty quiet about that. Still, that doesn't mean anything, surely?

'Forget Radio Basingstoke, we'll be on MTV this time next week!' I bluff. 'The youngest thrash-metal-punk band to go straight into the charts at number one!'

Murphy just sighs.

'We have to believe,' I tell him. 'We have to be confident!'

'I know,' he says. 'I am. It's just . . . well, I don't want to be too confident. And, Daizy . . . I just don't want you to be too disappointed if things don't work out.'

I just laugh.

'I won't be disappointed,' I promise, as Murphy slopes off across the street. 'And trust me – we can't lose!'

Last-minute nerves, that's all it is, I decide,

watching Murphy slouch along the street beneath
the streetlights. Everybody has those . . . right?

14

When the phone rings a few minutes later, I assume it is Murphy, still worried about the gig tomorrow. Becca takes the call . . . and it is definitely not Murphy.

'Who did you say you were?' my big sister asks carelessly. 'Dad? I don't think so. We don't have a dad any more. He ran away to Africa and never bothered to call. We think he may have been eaten by a lion, or crushed by a herd of elephants, and that means you are an imposter!'

Becca hands the phone to Pixie, smirking.

'Have you got me a honey badger?' my little sister demands. 'I've been building a hutch for one in the back garden. Do you think that I could feed it on hamster mix? Or would dog food be better?'

I grab the phone.

'Dad!' I squeal. 'You're alive!'

'Definitely,' Dad says, but his voice sounds very crackly and far away. 'I am at Lilongwe Airport, ready to catch my flight home!'

'Oh, Dad!' I tell him. 'We've been so worried! We thought you'd fallen down a well or died of malaria! Why didn't you ring?'

'My mobile ran out of battery and I'd forgotten to bring spares,' he explains. 'There was no electricity in the village to use a charger.'

'That's what Mum said,' I tell him.

She also said he was an irresponsible idiot living in a fantasy world, but I decide not to mention that bit.

'I have a lot to tell you,' I say brightly. 'I am a thrash-metal-punk guitarist now, and also a honey badger, but not the African kind, obviously. A different kind. You can come and see me tomorrow night at the Battle of the Bands and you'll see. I really think I have found my star quality this time, Dad!'

'That's my girl,' he laughs. 'You know what? I have missed you, Daizy Star!'

I feel a little catch in my throat. 'I've missed you too, Dad!' I say, but my voice comes out all snuffly and one perfect tear rolls down my cheek.

Mum takes the phone and starts talking briskly about flight times and pick-up arrangements. She could at least try to seem a little bit pleased.

I try to picture their reunion at the airport. Their eyes will meet across a crowded arrivals lounge, and they will realize how much they have missed each other and run into each other's arms, and everything will be sorted.

I hope.

But what if it isn't? What if Dad still wants to

live in Malawi and Mum says she's had enough and the late-night rows start up again? I don't want to think about that. I won't think about that.

My dad is coming home . . . tomorrow! It's almost more exciting than the Battle of the Bands.

I wake up next morning with a huge smile on my face. I could be on the edge of rock superstardom!

And best of all, Dad is coming home just in time to see it all happen.

Dad's flight is an overnight one, so he should be in the air right now. Mum is up bright and early, ready to head off to Heathrow to meet him.

'He won't be jet-lagged, will he?' I ask. 'He'll be OK to come to the Battle of the Bands?'

'He should be,' Mum sighs. 'He'll have all day to recover from the flight. Don't worry, Daizy.'

'I'm not worried!' I argue. 'Why does everybody think I am worried? Everything is going exactly according to plan.'

At school, the class is buzzing. Kelly, Freya and Luka have made a banner that reads *Honey Badgers Forever*. Miss Moon says she has got a front-row seat. Even Ethan has a ticket . . . and he asks if we'd like him to turn up early to help with the guitars and amps and stuff.

Yeah, right.

I give him a withering look. 'You don't have to turn up at all, Ethan,' I say coldly. 'Haven't you got something more important to do? Like polishing your football boots, or practising your goal-scoring techniques, or dropping worms down people's sweatshirts?'

Ethan looks sad. 'Daizy, that worm thing was years ago,' he sighs. 'We were in Year Three, and I've said I'm sorry about a million times since then. You have to forgive me sometime, y'know.'

I raise an eyebrow frostily. 'Wanna bet?' I ask.

'Ethan, she doesn't mean it!' Beth cuts in. 'Daizy is just stressed because of the pressure and everything. Of course she forgives you, and she definitely wants you to come along tonight. We all do, don't we?'

'I do, Ethan,' Willow breathes. 'I'm counting on it. I'll be watching out for you! And you're just sooooo good at all that technical stuff, so maybe you could hang out with us beforehand and help me tweak my mike and my amp. That would be amazing!'

'Er, right,' Ethan says with a smirk. 'See you there then.' My two best friends are seriously embarrassing whenever Ethan is around. It must be their hormones bubbling away and turning their brains into mush. Growing up can be a very scary thing.

I check my watch. Dad will be home by now. He and Mum will be drinking tea and sharing stories about life in the African sun. And very soon they will be sitting side by side at the Battle of the Bands, watching The Honey Badgers win, and they will be filled with pride and happiness.

We will be a happy family again. When I hand

over the £500 cheque to Dad he will send it off to Malawi and then his conscience will be clear and the nightmare will be over. That's what I am hoping, anyway.

Our very last practice in the school music room is pretty impressive, if I do say so myself. We rock, in a deafening kind of way. Willow has perfected the art of the thrash-punk-metal screech, and Beth's drumming sounds exactly like a washing machine full of gravel, on full spin. Murphy is brilliant on bass, and my guitar riffs are loud enough to lift the roof off.

We are almost ready.

All that is needed now is Becca's thrash-punk-metal makeover skills.

After school, the four of us, with Pixie in tow, trail back to number 17, Silver Street. Everyone is excited, but I am just about bursting with happiness because Dad will be back and I cannot wait to see him. At the corner of the street, I break into a run and I don't stop until I am hurtling through the front door into the hallway.

There is no sign of either Mum or Dad cuddled up on the sofa the way I hoped they might be. There is no sign of them at all.

'Dad!' I yell. 'Dad! Mum? Where are you?'

Becca appears on the staircase.

'They're not here,' she tells me. 'Dad's plane was delayed in Lilongwe . . . Mum's been stuck at the airport all day, waiting for him. She rang my mobile to say we are not to worry, Dad is definitely on his way now. They should make it in time for the Battle of the Bands, but they might have to go straight there.'

'What?' I yelp. 'But . . . Dad was meant to be here hours ago! What if they miss my moment of glory?'

Becca ruffles my hair. 'It'll all work out, Daizy,' she says. 'Don't worry. Come on, help me get my make-up kit and crimpers set up . . . we have work to do!'

By the time Pixie, Beth, Willow and Murphy arrive, Becca and I have turned the living room into a thrash-punk-metal beauty salon. I get to work crimping Beth's hair while Becca starts painting Willow's eyes and nails a startling shade of neon green. There is lots of inky eyeliner and black lipstick that makes us look faintly vampire-ish.

Next, we get changed into the splash-painted T-shirts and little black skirts, or skinny red jeans in Murphy's case, and Becca gets to work on our hair. She gives Pixie a handful of neon hair mascaras, and soon random stripes of turquoise, orange and pink appear in everyone's hair. Becca starts backcombing madly and scooshing us with great clouds of hairspray, adding black lace bows and scarves to go with the black furry ears.

Murphy gets a whole crop of pointy dinosaur spikes all over the back of his head while his dipping, multi-coloured fringe is straightened. Becca even threatens him with the black eyeliner, but he wriggles away before she can do any damage.

We are ready. We have through-a-hedge-backwards hair and panda eyes, and clothes that look like Halloween fancy dress.

'Scary,' Pixie says, and I agree. If I saw the whole bunch of us walking along Silver Street, I would turn round and leg it in the opposite direction.

We look perfect.

But there is a little ache of sadness in my chest because it's five thirty now and time to set off for Brightford Playhouse, and there is still no sign of Dad. If he doesn't hurry up, he's going to miss our big break.

Becca slips an arm round my shoulder. 'Stop worrying,' she whispers. 'He'll be there.'

'I know,' I say, but I don't believe it. My confidence has dissolved. A feeling of doom and disaster is hanging over me. There's the toot of a car horn from outside, and we grab the guitars and load them into Murphy's mum's car. We don't have to stress about drum kits and mikes and amps because Spike's band are bringing theirs along and all the bands will be sharing them once we get to the theatre.

All that's left is for us to squeeze into the car and go, and suddenly my tummy is full of butterflies because it's not every day you get to achieve your thrash-punk-metal potential and change the world as well, all in ten short minutes on stage. It is going to be *awesome*.

I just hope Mum and Dad will be there to see it.

Once we get to the theatre, things get a little scary. We have a bit of trouble convincing the sound-check guys we are actually a band and not a bunch of autograph-hunting fans trying to sneak backstage, which is very ageist of them when you think about it. In the end, Spike spots us and vouches for us, and then we are up there with the other bands, who do seem very tall and old and scary-looking.

Beth and Willow have gone totally silent, and Murphy just keeps saying, 'Right, cool,' whenever someone asks him a question.

One of the sound-check crew takes a look at Murphy's bass and my pink guitar, and wires them up to a couple of huge amps on the stage.

'These are pretty powerful . . . give them a go,' he suggests.

'Right, cool!' Murphy says.

We play a few chords. The sound-check guy twiddles with the amps and the sound that comes out is pretty ear-splitting. Beth tries the drums and manages to lose a drumstick and pull one of the hi-hat cymbals down on top of her. She is shaking like a leaf and looks like she might cry at any minute.

'You'll be OK,' the sound-check guy tells us. 'It's normal to be nervous before a gig. Trust me, once you're playing, you'll be buzzed!'

'Right, cool!'

I dig Murphy in the ribs with a sharp elbow. He is getting seriously annoying.

'Anyway, let me know if there's anything else you need,' the sound-check guy says. 'You're tenth in the running order, so you're actually last on. I'll call you five minutes before. I'll take you to the green room to relax. We open in ten minutes . . .'

He leads us through to the green room, which is a poky, scabby little dressing room that isn't even green, and tells us to wait in there. It is like a sardine can, only with weirdos instead of fish inside it. There is a boy with a purple Mohican and a girl with tattooed arms that look like lacy blue sleeves and a bloke with a shaved head and an orange beard trained into two pointy plaits.

Spike appears out of the madness, looking fairly harmless compared to the others, even with his pierced lip and green hair.

'OK, Daizy?' he grins.

My mouth has gone very dry. I try to answer, but all that comes out is a croak.

We follow Spike into the sardine can and he hands us cans of lemonade from a crate in the corner. 'Keep your energy levels up,' he says.

I slurp down some of the lemonade and I start to feel fizzy inside – fizzy and excited. It's really, really happening . . . and so much depends on this.

I find myself wondering again if Dad's plane has landed yet. Will he make it on time?

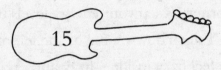 **15**

Things happen fast after that. The sound-check guy calls up the first band, and we can hear cheers from the auditorium and the heavy thumping of the bass and drums.

'I don't like this,' Beth whispers. 'I've changed my mind. I want to go home!'

'Too bad,' I tell her. 'You promised!'

'But, Daizy –'

'But nothing,' I say. 'This is no time to get cold feet. Think of all those poor children in Malawi, with no school books and no proper shoes and nothing but deep-fried mouse fritters for special occasions.'

Beth is starting to look a little green. Maybe I

shouldn't have mentioned the mouse fritters.

'Think of me,' I plead. 'Think of my family. This is the only thing that can save us!'

'Think of Ethan Miller,' Willow snaps, and Beth blinks and nods and stands up a little straighter.

'OK,' she says in a shaky voice. 'I can do this. For Ethan Miller, I can do it.'

Ethan Miller? Urghhh. Now I am starting to feel a little queasy, but I grip my can of lemonade and take a sip, and all thoughts of Ethan ebb away.

One by one, the bands are on, and finally Spike's band is playing, and that is deeply scary because it means we are next. The sound-check guy comes to fetch us and we wait in the wings as The Smashed Bananas finish their set, and even I can see they are pretty amazing. In fact, they are more than amazing, they are eye-poppingly awesome and ear-splittingly stunning. For the first time, I begin to panic.

The Smashed Bananas are brilliant. They dive

around the stage, they leap, they jump, they slide, they spin. The lead singer leans down towards the audience and Spike does this thing where he rocks the guitar backwards and forward and then jumps into the air with this random karate high-kick kind of move. It is impressive.

I didn't realize how good Spike's band really are. They have the audience rocking. A crowd of teenagers have swarmed down to the front of the stage, in front of the seats, and are moshing and jumping about in time to the music.

My tummy flips over. The Smashed Bananas will be very hard to beat.

The Honey Badgers do not leap, kick, slide or spin.

We haven't even thought of that. Usually, we just kind of stand there, clutching our instruments anxiously, and keeping a lookout for Mr Bleecher. It's not going to be a winning look, I can see that now.

'Try to move,' I whisper to the others urgently. 'Jiggle about a bit, or kick, or jump into the air. Go wild.'

Willow rolls her eyes, Murphy just looks at me as if I am crazy, and Beth is shaking so much I'm not sure she'll be able to hold her drumsticks.

And then The Smashed Bananas have finished and the audience go crazy, and Spike grins and ruffles my hair as he strides off the stage.

'Break a leg, Daizy Star!' he says.

'What?' I gasp, horrified, and Willow has to explain that this is what performers say when they are wishing each other luck before going on stage, and that it is traditional.

And then we are walking on to the stage, into the bright white spotlight, and I realize too late that I am still clutching the can of lemonade, so I put it down carefully on the nearest speaker, plug in the pink guitar and turn towards the audience.

It's dark out there, but I can see a big blur of faces. More people than you get in assembly at Stella Street Primary, that's for sure. The teenagers at the front are standing still, wiping their foreheads and waiting for us to rock their world. Somewhere in the middle, a banner that reads *Honey Badgers Forever* is waving around, and in the front row of seats I catch sight of Ted Tingley, looking very serious and jotting things down in a notebook. I scan the crowd for a sign of Mum and Dad, but the only familiar faces I see are Miss Moon, Ethan Miller and, bizarrely, Mr Bleecher the school caretaker, complete with earmuffs. Scary.

'Ready?' Murphy whispers.

And then I hear a yell from the audience. 'Go for it, Daizy Star!' and right at the back I see a skinny bloke in a crumpled T-shirt, with a very, very red face. *Dad!*

I play the first few chords of 'Get My Goat', and Murphy is with me on bass and even Beth is hammering away at the drums. Willow begins to sing . . . well, screech, really.

> *I don't want an Xbox, an iPod or a Wii,*
> *I don't want a skateboard beneath the Christmas tree,*
> *I live in Malawi where life is proud and free,*
> *I don't want your western ways, or your charity!*

I just want a chance to live the way I choose,
And maybe an old bicycle, or just a pair of shoes . . .
A well with clean, fresh water and a plate that's full of rice,
Plenty of fruit and vegetables and no more deep-fried mice.
One thing more than anything would really get my vote,
Let this be the Christmas I really get my goat!

We all join in with the chorus:

A herd of goats, a herd of goats,
A herd of goats to call my own . . .
If you have a herd of goats,
You'll never be alone!

As the last chorus dies away, the audience seems stunned into silence. Someone at the back starts to clap, a little uncertainly.

A trickle of doubt slides down my spine.

What if guitar is *not* my star quality after all? What if the Honey Badgers are not going to be the superstars of tomorrow?

What if we don't win?

'Come on, Daizy!' Dad yells from the back, and suddenly it doesn't matter whether we win or not . . . it just matters that we do our best.

I launch into the next song, skipping about a bit as I strum. 'Dance!' I hiss at Willow and Murphy. 'Please! For me!'

Willow grabs the mike from its stand and starts jumping about as she sings, and Murphy makes a couple of hops and shuffles. The audience are thawing a little now – only a few of them have their hands over their ears.

By the time we start our final song, 'My Dad's Mid-life Crisis', I know there is no option but to give it all I've got. I remember Spike's karate kicks, and I leap into the air and finish with a skid that takes me right up to the edge of the stage. I might have gone right over, but my guitar is still plugged in, and the cord jerks me back from the brink. There is a crackle of feedback and the sound-check guy starts waving his arms around frantically.

I think he likes it.

And the teenagers at the front are really moshing now, shaking their heads about and waving their arms in the air. I am lost in the music, my fingers raw, my heart racing, my hair a tangle of curls that fall across my face.

I try for a jump, a kick and a spin, and for a moment – one fantastic, glorious moment – I am flying, and the pink guitar is singing, and my whole body fizzes with excitement.

It doesn't last for long.

Spinning around with an electric guitar in your hands is not a good plan. The guitar lead wraps itself round my legs and I stagger backwards, clattering into the snare drum and pulling the crash cymbal down on top of me.

I try to stand upright, but my legs are hobbled by the guitar cord and I lurch forward, teetering on the edge of the stage like a tightrope walker struggling for balance.

The grungy teenagers at the front are still now, and silent, their mouths open in horror. Willow's voice trails off to a whimper, Beth freezes with her drumsticks in mid-air, and Murphy shrugs off his bass guitar and reaches out to grab me, but it's all too late because I wobble dangerously for a split second and then plummet down into the crowd.

It's a bit like when I was learning to swim. I just know I am going to drown, only this time it is in a sea of sweaty strangers and not the local swimming pool. I will crash to the floor and be trampled by a thousand moshing feet in Doc Marten boots. I might as well do it in style. I scream and spread my arms out wide and close my eyes tight shut as I fall . . .

And a hundred hands reach up to save me, holding me safe above the crowd, passing me

across the heads of the scrum of scruffy teens.
I am passed from hand to hand gently, like a
parcel filled with something fragile.

And then, finally, I reach the edge of the
auditorium and someone lowers me down, and
I am sandwiched right between Miss Moon and
Ted Tingley.

'Daizy, Daizy, are you all right?' Miss Moon is
saying.

'What the heck were you doing?' Ted Tingley
demands. 'Stage-diving and crowd-surfing are
very dangerous tricks to play! That's expensive

equipment up there – you could have blown
something up! You could have wrecked the amp,
shorted the speaker, smashed your guitar . . .'

'You could have hurt yourself, Daizy,' Miss
Moon says kindly.

I feel as though I have been kicked and
battered and beaten, or trampled by a herd of
wild goats. I bet I have about a million bruises all
over my body.

'I'm OK,' I say in a small voice.

And then I look up at the stage. Beth,
Willow and Murphy are huddled together,

open-mouthed. Drums and cymbals and Murphy's bass guitar are scattered like wreckage across the stage, and on the big speaker my can of lemonade has fallen over and is dripping steadily down. I frown. That's a bad thing. I'm sure somebody told me that things like that were dangerous . . .

As I watch, the speaker crackles, fizzes and then explodes like a basketful of fireworks on the fifth of November. Blue sparks fly out from it in every direction and plumes of black smoke billow into the air. My eyes widen in horror and my mouth forms a perfect 'o' of dismay.

And then the whole speaker explodes into flames, with a *bang* that sends the whole audience running, screaming, for the exits.

Oops.

16

Of course, by the time the fire brigade has gone, most of the audience have lost interest, given up and gone home. There are only a few stragglers left to file back into the auditorium and listen while Ted Tingley and his fellow judges announce the winners.

I know I have blown our chances . . . any hopes of winning that prize went up in smoke at exactly the same moment the speaker did. But still, there is a little part of me that cannot stop hoping for a miracle.

I mean, it's not as if I *planned* to set the stage on fire. Not literally, anyhow.

I stand in a huddle with Willow, Beth and

Murphy, with Mum, Dad, Becca, Pixie and the other families close by. Miss Moon and Ethan Miller are waiting too, loyal to the end.

Ted Tingley walks up on to the stage. It's a little bit slippery from all that foam stuff the firefighters squirted everywhere, but hardly any of the stage is actually charred. Ted clears his throat.

'Tonight's Battle of the Bands is perhaps one of the most memorable gigs we will ever attend,' he says, shooting me a dark look. 'Stage-diving, fireworks, an impromptu smoke machine . . . some new bands will do anything to grab the limelight.'

My face flames. Is Ted Tingley talking about The Honey Badgers? Doesn't he know it was an accident? Can't he see it was a mistake? Dad puts his hands on my shoulders gently and that makes me feel less alone.

'We are not interested in gimmicks,' Ted Tingley goes on ominously. 'We are interested in raw, new talent. We are interested in originality, personality and style. We are looking for cutting-edge new songs, brilliant guitar skills, beat and rhythm, and rock and roll. And with those things in mind, one band stands out above all of the others . . .'

My heart starts to thud. We are original. We have personality and style. I'm sure we do. Is it totally crazy to still hope? Willow and Beth, on either side of me, slip their hands into mine, and Murphy just winks.

'The winners are . . .' Ted Tingley glances around the auditorium, and silence falls across us like a warm blanket, 'The Smashed Bananas!'

My heart sinks right to the bottom of my red Converse trainers, and my eyes brim with tears. Becca is hugging Spike, and then my sister's boyfriend and his band run up on to the stage and accept their prize.

I am happy for Spike, really I am.
I clap as loud and as long as I can, but my heart is breaking, and it's all my own fault. My dreams are in little

pieces – a bit like the ruined speaker
– and my future is bleak.

I am destined to be a failed thrash-punk-metal
princess, living in Malawi, in a village without
electricity. The pink guitar will grow dusty and
neglected. It will blister in the scorching sun, and
the glossy pink paintwork will peel and flake.
Tropical spiders will weave webs round it, and
eventually, Dad will use it to patch up a hole in
the corner of our hut.

Either that, or else Mum will divorce Dad, and
Becca will run off to join the circus with Spike.
It'll just be Pixie and me, two abandoned sisters
from a broken home. Pixie will probably never
believe in the tooth fairy, or Father Christmas, or
mermaids, ever again. And I will never find my
star quality, not ever.

'I've ruined everything,' I snuffle. 'I was only
trying to help, but I've wrecked it all! What a
disaster!'

'I don't know,' Murphy says. 'I thought it was
fun. Maybe we didn't win, but you didn't really

think we would, did you, Daizy? Not really and truly?'

I open my mouth to argue and close it again, blinking. I really and truly did.

'But if I hadn't messed up . . .'

Murphy shrugs. 'The judges seemed to think it was all part of the act,' he says. 'Apart from the actual explosion, of course.'

'Don't mention the explosion,' I groan.

'You could say our set went out with a real bang,' Willow says.

'We were unforgettable,' Beth smirks.

'The light show was awesome!' Murphy chips in.

Well, it's all right for them. The band was never a matter of life or death for Murphy, Willow and Beth. For me, it was . . . and without that prize money, I have no solution, no answers, no plan that will stop Dad whisking us all away to Malawi. Or worse, stop my family from falling apart.

'Well done, Daizy,' Miss Moon says kindly.

'You may not have won, but you have done something very special here tonight. You have made people think . . . about Malawi. You have made *me* think. I am very proud of you, Daizy Star.'

'It was cool,' Beth says.

'It was crazy,' Willow agrees.

'I liked the one about the goat,' Ethan chips in. 'I think I told you – my uncle has a goat farm.'

I roll my eyes.

Then Spike is coming back down from the stage, and he walks across and shakes my hand and I smile as hard as I can and tell him that he was brilliant and that the best band won.

'Well, we were a bit more experienced,' he says. 'But I think The Honey Badgers have real potential.'

And then he does an amazing thing. He hands me a roll of tenners, and when I look it turns out to be £100, Spike's share of the £500 prize money. 'For Malawi,' he says. 'Becca told me what you were trying to do.'

And I hug Spike because
he may be big and
scary with a pierced
lip and green hair,
and he may have
snatched my dream
of stardom right from
under my nose, but he is
definitely one of the coolest
people I know.

I turn to Dad and hand him the roll of notes.
'This is for you,' I tell him. 'For the school in
Malawi. Or . . . well, something, anyway. I
didn't win the whole five hundred pounds, but
if I had . . .'

Dad grins. 'I know, Daizy, I know,' he says.
'Come on. Time to go home.'

The thing about hanging around in dark theatres
and dimly lit street corners is that they're . . . dark
and dimly lit. You just can't see very well.

So, it's not until we
get back home and
Dad takes off his
jacket and scarf and
floppy hat, that I really get
a proper look at him. My
eyes widen in horror.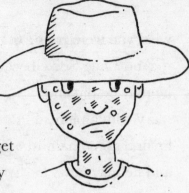

His skin is pink and peeling, with raised red
bumps all over it.

'Yeughhh!' Pixie exclaims. 'Have you got
chicken pox?'

'Plague, more like,' Becca says. 'Is it
contagious?'

'Is it . . . is it fatal?' I choke out.

Dad just laughs. 'It's none of those things,' he
tells us. 'I just have a bad case of sunburn . . .
and it turns out I am allergic to mosquito bites.'

'What are the chances?' Mum sighs.

'It's very annoying,' Dad says. 'Malawi was
wonderful, but it was very, very hot, and the
mosquitoes were a nightmare. I don't think I
could live there.'

My heart leaps. 'You couldn't?' I gasp. 'You mean . . . we don't have to go to live in Malawi after all?'

Dad looks guilty. 'I don't think it would be fair to uproot you all and take you to Malawi,' he sighs. 'It wouldn't be right to do that. It was my dream, after all, my idea . . .'

'Does that mean you might go *without* us?' I ask, alarmed.

'No, no, of course not, Daizy!' Dad protests. 'Why would I do that? I missed you all, every minute I was away. More than three weeks . . . well, it would have been awful!'

I take a deep breath in, and the butterflies in my tummy start to settle at last.

'To be honest,' Dad sighs, 'I was pretty hopeless. The heat made me feel ill, my skin peeled like crazy and the mosquito allergy was just the last straw. Besides . . . I am not sure digging wells and plastering walls is really my skill.'

'I could have told you that,' Becca says.

Dad sighs. 'I think I may have been a bit of a liability when it came to the practical stuff. I still think I'd have enjoyed the teaching, but . . . well, the truth is, I wasn't really suited to life in Malawi. I don't think I had thought it through.'

'Obviously,' Mum says with a little smile. 'Never mind, Mike. It's probably for the best.'

'Probably,' Dad admits, and he looks very sad, in a red and peely kind of a way.

'So, we're not going?' Pixie asks. 'But I had my heart set on having a honey badger of my very own. Maybe I could have a pet rabbit instead? For Christmas?'

'Maybe,' Dad says weakly.

I don't say anything. I just fling my arms round Dad and hug him very, very tightly because miracles really do happen after all.

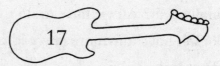

17

D ad decides that the best way he can help the children of Malawi is by staying safely on British soil. He starts to help out on the charity website, advising would-be volunteers on what to expect in Africa.

'It's not as easy as you imagine, saving the world,' he sighs.

'No,' Mum agrees. 'But you had a good try, Mike. I'm proud of you, in a funny kind of a way.'

Mum and Dad seem to be getting on a lot better, now that the threat of life in a straw-thatched hut is no longer looming. I am very glad about that.

'You have helped to dig a well and build a school,' Mum says kindly. 'You've made a real difference. That's what you wanted, isn't it?'

'I guess so,' Dad says. 'There are all kinds of different ways to help. I can see that now.'

Who knows, maybe Dad's mid-life crisis is finally over? All we have to do is make sure he doesn't have any more crazy ideas. How hard can it be?

We send off Spike's £100 and the charity send us a letter to say they will use it to buy school books, pens and paper, so I guess that the Battle of the Bands was worth it in the end. Kind of.

Back at school, Miss Moon tells me that she wants to twin Stella Street Primary with the new school in Tatu Mtengo. She rings Dad a few times and contacts the charity Dad volunteered with, and she starts planning a whole new project for the New Year, a way for the two schools to learn from each other and share resources and help each other out. And Class Six might even get pen pals in Malawi, which is going to be pretty cool.

I stop going for guitar lessons with Ted Tingley. Dad says he doesn't seem very chilled out for a guitar guru, and Mum says he didn't really appreciate my talents anyhow. I am sad about that, but Spike says he will show me the basics and I keep on practising with the pink guitar, even though I secretly know that it is not going to be my star quality after all.

It's still fun, even if I am not very good.

The weirdest thing that happens is that on the last day of term, I get a Christmas card from Ethan Miller. It is a card with sparkly, glittery snow and a cartoon robin on it, and I cannot even show it to Beth or Willow because Ethan does not bother giving a card to them.

This is kind of scary.

Inside the card, there is a message:

Happy Cristmus, Daizy Star, lotz of luv, Ethan xxxx
P.S. I have got a Cristmus prezzie for the children in Malawi. Meet me by the tyre-swing in the park, today at 6 o'clock.

I am not going to go, obviously. Only a crazy person would agree to meet Ethan Miller by the tyre-swing, especially after dark on the last day of term.

Then again, he has a prezzie for the kids in Malawi. Maybe he really does have a heart? Maybe he has raised some money by holding a sponsored football match, or sold his hair gel and his flashy trainers to buy plastic buckets or maize seeds or a first-aid kit. He did give me an old football and an old footy kit after all.

Perhaps I have misjudged Ethan Miller. Or perhaps he just wants to get me alone, so he can chase me with a worm.

'Becca?' I ask, at five to six that evening. 'What would you do if a really, really annoying boy wanted to meet you by the tyre-swing in the park?'

Becca raises an eyebrow. 'Daizy, you are too young to have a boyfriend,' she says primly.

I pretend to stick my fingers down my throat. 'Bleughhh!' I say. 'That's just sick! I do not want a boyfriend, not ever, and if I did it would not be Ethan Miller, trust me. But he says he has a prezzie for the kids in Malawi. What should I do?'

'When does he want to meet you, exactly?' Becca frowns.

'Now!'

Becca, Pixie and me leg it down to the park. Pixie brings her mermaid torch, which works underwater, but doesn't seem to work very well out of it. I spot a shadowy figure lurking by the tyre-swing.

'Yell if he tries any funny business,' Becca says. 'I'll break both his legs.'

'I'll break both his arms,' Pixie adds.

I almost feel sorry for Ethan Miller. Almost, but not quite.

Then I hear a terrifying sound, a harsh, guttural cry like an old man choking, or a goat with a bad cough. It sends a shiver down my spine. Perhaps the shadowy figure is not Ethan at all, but a mad axe-murderer?

'Daizy!' Ethan says. 'At last! I thought you'd never get here!'

I'm beginning to wish I hadn't. 'What was that noise?' I whisper.

'Oh, that was Buttercup,' Ethan says casually. 'I wanted to get you something really cool for Christmas, Daizy. Something to make up for the worm incident back in Year Three. Something to show you I am not a loser or an idiot.'

'Er . . . right,' I say.

I don't think there is anything in the world that can do that, but I don't want to hurt Ethan's feelings.

'I thought very hard,' Ethan sighs. 'And I decided that getting you something for those kids in Malawi would be the right thing to do. And of course, your song at the Battle of the Bands gave me the idea. So . . . here she is. Buttercup!'

There is a rustling noise, and a tiny bundle of fur leaps through the darkness and bashes me on the leg. It's like a mad dog, or a frantic, outsize, killer-cat. Or . . .

'It's a goat!' I yell, as Buttercup takes a bite out of my school skirt and starts to chew. *'Help!'*

Becca and Pixie are beside me in a heartbeat, but instead of breaking Ethan's arms and legs, as promised, they fall on the baby goat, fussing, petting, stroking.

'Actually, it's a kid. For Malawi,' Ethan explains. 'You said that a herd of goats can make a whole village independent. And like I said, my uncle has a goat farm. So . . .'

Words fail me. Ethan Miller is grinning at me through the darkness. Seriously, has there ever been a more idiotic boy in the history of the world?

'Ethan,' I say as patiently as I can manage. 'Malawi is in Africa. And Buttercup is here. Think about it. We would have to buy her a plane ticket, stick her on a plane and then arrange to get her driven a couple of hundred miles across Malawi to get to Tatu Mtengo. It would cost hundreds and hundreds of pounds. We could buy a whole herd of goats, for that. *African* goats.'

'Oh . . .' Ethan says. 'I didn't think of that.'

'No,' I say sharply. 'You never think at all.'

'She's quite cute, though,' Becca says.

'I have always wanted a pet goat,' Pixie adds.

Ethan sighs. 'Shall I take her away?' he asks sadly. 'Tell my uncle you don't want her?'

'No!' Pixie wails. 'We'll keep her!'

'We can't,' I huff. 'Where would she sleep?'

'My room,' Pixie grins.

'The shed in the garden,' Becca suggests. 'You can't send her back to the farm, Daizy. She might end up in a pie or a stew or a tin of dog food or something. Farming is a cut-throat business.'

'My uncle just makes cheese,' Ethan says
defensively.

I kneel down and look Buttercup in the eye.
It's kind of disturbing. Her eyes are kind of
yellowish and spooky. And then she leans forward
and starts nuzzling my hair and chewing one of
my plaits, and I know there's no way I can send
her back to the farm.

'We'll keep her,' Becca decides. 'Say thank
you, Daizy!'

'Thanks, Ethan,' I say grudgingly, and Ethan
laughs and says he knew I'd get my goat one day.
He takes off into the darkness.

We are busy making Buttercup a nest in the
kitchen from old pillows and blankets when Mum
and Dad get home from late-night Christmas
shopping. I try to explain, but Mum is not
impressed.

'She was a present,' I say. 'You can't refuse a
present, can you?'

'We cannot keep a goat, Daizy,' Mum says.

'No way. Not happening. And definitely not in the house. Is that clear?'

'Dad?' I appeal.

Dad narrows his eyes. He looks at Buttercup, and very slowly, a smile spreads over his face.

'Don't worry, girls,' he says. 'I've just had a *brilliant* idea!'

It all started with a Scarecrow.

Puffin is seventy years old.

Sounds ancient, doesn't it? But Puffin has never been
so lively. We're always on the lookout for the next big
idea, which is how it began all those years ago.

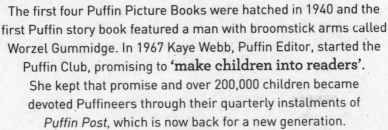

Penguin Books was a big idea from the mind of
a man called Allen Lane, who in 1935 invented
the quality paperback and changed the world.
**And from great Penguins, great Puffins grew,
changing the face of children's books forever.**

The first four Puffin Picture Books were hatched in 1940 and the
first Puffin story book featured a man with broomstick arms called
Worzel Gummidge. In 1967 Kaye Webb, Puffin Editor, started the
Puffin Club, promising to **'make children into readers'**.
She kept that promise and over 200,000 children became
devoted Puffineers through their quarterly instalments of
Puffin Post, which is now back for a new generation.

Many years from now, we hope you'll look back and
remember Puffin with a smile. **No matter what your age
or what you're into, there's a Puffin for everyone.**
The possibilities are endless, but one thing is for sure:
whether it's a picture book or a paperback, a sticker book
or a hardback, **if it's got that little Puffin
on it – it's bound to be good.**